THE BEDROOM ASSIGNMENT

THE BEDROOM ASSIGNMENT

BY

SOPHIE WESTON

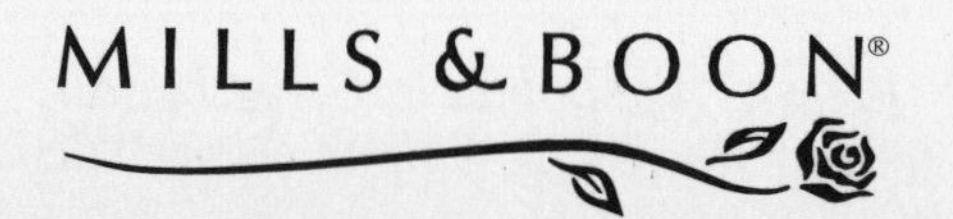

First published in Great Britain 2002
Large Print edition 2003
Harlequin Mills & Boon Limited,
Eton House, 18-24 Paradise Road,
Richmond, Surrey TW9 1SR

ISBN 0 263 17872 2

Set in Times Roman 15½ on 16½ pt.
16-0103-55302

Printed and bound in Great Britain
by Antony Rowe Ltd, Chippenham, Wiltshire

CHAPTER ONE

'THERE'S more to relationships than sex, Zo,' announced her best friend with energy. 'You've got to be a bit more flexible.'

In the act of filling the kettle, Zoe Brown looked up and stared in disbelief. 'I beg your pardon?' she said. 'Where did that come from?'

Suze had rushed into the old-fashioned kitchen like a whirlwind, casting her briefcase to one side and her shopping bags to the other. She had not even sat down before she launched her bombshell. Now she perched on the settle against the wall with a small, complacent smile.

'I don't know what it is that Simon's done...' She paused expectantly.

Zoe cast her eyes to heaven. 'Is there anything you don't think is your business? What did you do? Stake out my house? Tap my phone?'

Suze grinned. But she was not to be deflected. 'Don't be coy. I don't have to spy on you to know what you're up to. We have no secrets.'

If only you knew, Suze.

Zoe found she had over-filled the kettle. She emptied some water out, and then switched the thing on before turning back to her friend.

'I knew something was wrong,' Suze announced loftily. Then added, with a slight diminution of ineffability, 'Besides, Simon called me.'

Well, that figured, thought Zoe. Suze had introduced her and Simon Frobisher in the first place. Simon was a member of Suze's Young Business Network. It was natural that he should confide in her when his fledgling romance with Zoe hit the buffers.

'Have you two had a row?'

'Not really,' said Zoe uncomfortably. 'We talked, but—'

Suze sighed theatrically. 'You talked!' she echoed. 'And another one bites the dust! I don't *believe* you.'

Zoe looked away. 'Is he very upset?' she said with compunction.

Suze pursed her lips. 'Confused is probably a better word,' she pronounced.

'I'm sorry about that.'

'It's understandable. He's a scarce commodity and he knows it. Single, straight, solvent. *And* a business that's going to make him a millionaire in the next five years. From his point of view, it's a seller's market.'

Zoe felt slightly better. 'You mean he isn't breaking his heart?'

In contrast to Zoe, who was barefoot in dusty cut-offs and a torn tee shirt, Suze was dressed in a business suit. But she kicked her legs against the settle like the five-year-old she had been when they'd first met at kindergarten.

'No, but he's scratching his head. He muttered something about sex...' Again Suze left an inviting pause.

'Did he?' Zoe's tone was discouraging.

'Aw, come on, Zo. Give.'

'Have a coffee,' said Zoe firmly.

She made instant coffee in two thick china mugs and padded across the kitchen with them. Suze took hers, but she frowned with irritation.

'I mean, you can't keep going through men like they grow on trees.' Her voice was full of righteous indignation. 'Quite apart from anything else, it's not fair to the rest of us.'

Zoe gave a hollow laugh. 'Is that right?'

Suze did not notice it was hollow. 'And it's beastly inconvenient. I never know who you're going to bring to a party.'

Zoe pushed back her untidy brown curls and hitched herself up onto the corner of the cluttered table. 'Well, if that's all you're worried about—'

'Or if you're going to bring anyone at all. And what he will be like if you do.'

'I'll make sure to send you the next one's resumé,' Zoe said dryly.

Suze Manoir grinned. 'Or you could just stick to the same man for more than a couple of dates,' she suggested. 'That would be a first.'

Oh, Lord, thought Zoe. Aloud she said, 'Yes, ma'am.'

'Oh, *you*,' said Suze, exasperated. 'Okay. I'll mind my own business. What do we need to do to get this house sorted?'

'Just about everything,' said Zoe wryly. 'Starting with rewiring and moving on up.'

The kitchen of the Brown family house was big and untidy. Just at the moment about a third of it looked beautiful. A wild green arrangement of leafy summer branches and ferns hid the peeling paintwork round the fireplace and the stains on the old pine table. Zoe had set out dishes of roast beef, and the Thai chicken and vegetable salads that she had prepared yesterday, all covered in plastic wrap. She had even set little groups of solid candles, ready for lighting, on the fireplace and one corner of the table.

But that was the far end of the kitchen. The other two thirds, where they were sitting, looked like a shipwreck. A pretty shabby shipwreck at that, thought Zoe ruefully.

She and her sister had slapped a coat of paint on the walls at Christmas, just to make it look more cheerful. But the whole house had a patched and mended air. Whereas Suze had shown an interior decorator round her central London pad for a television lifestyle programme, and the Manoir house was immaculately presented.

Suze followed her eyes. 'Hey,' she said gently, showing that in this area, at least, she was right that they had no secrets. 'So it's a bit battered. Don't worry about it. That's why we're having the party here, after all.'

'Good point,' agreed Zoe. 'Okay, let's kick back and party.'

From the moment that they'd taken charge of their own birthday celebrations, Suze and Zoe had given a joint party at Zoe's house. They chose a day in the summer, when hopefully people would be able to go out into the garden, and called it their Official Birthday. Suze said that the arrangement gave her more freedom than her parents' house and more room than her own flat. But Zoe knew it was more than that.

Suze knew that, ever since Zoe's father had left home, money had been dreadfully tight—and, even worse, that Zoe's mother had withdrawn into the cocoon of her own world. The Official Birthday Party was Suze's way of helping out without admitting it.

'You're a good friend,' Zoe said with affection.

She went over to the big wipe-down board where the family left messages for each other. Today it had been wiped clear—no phone messages for Artemis, her twenty-year-old younger sister, currently out with boyfriend Ed, or notes about washing seventeen-year-old Harry's rugby kit. Today it was covered by one orderly list in Zoe's neat writing. More than half the items had already been ticked off.

'You're so efficient,' said Suze with a sigh. She came up and stood at Zoe's shoulder. 'You're really wasted here. You ought to be running a government, not this mad house.'

Zoe flung up a hand.

'Oh, all right,' said Suze, as she always did. 'You know your own business best. Got a job for next week?'

Zoe pulled a face. 'Just a couple of guided walks along the Thames. I'll probably call the library department on Monday morning, see if they've got anyone sick.'

'I wish you'd sign on with me again,' Suze said wistfully. She ran her own very successful staff agency. 'People are always asking for you.'

'Maybe after the summer,' said Zoe vaguely. She narrowed her eyes at the list. 'Put up fairy lights in the apple tree. Glitter balls in the sitting room. Which do you want to do?'

'Sounds like manual labour.' Suze looked at her elegantly painted fingernails and shuddered. 'We'll do them together,' she decreed.

They went out into the garden first. Zoe brought the ladder out of the shed and slung it over her shoulder to carry it up to the orchard.

'High-ho, high-ho,' sang Suze, following behind with a coil of outdoor fairy lights.

Zoe grinned over her shoulder. 'I'm no dwarf.'

It was true. She was nearly as tall as her six-foot father, and certainly as striking, with her candid, wide-open brown eyes and mop of unruly chestnut curls.

'No, but you're certainly one of the workers of the world,' said Suze, watching as Zoe lodged the ladder against the tree trunk in a workmanlike manner. 'Now, if Simon were here he could do it. That's what men are for.'

Zoe pushed a dusty brown curl behind her ear and measured the angle of the ladder. She adjusted it.

'Well, Simon's not coming,' she said bracingly. 'Get used to it. And hang onto the ladder. You don't have to chip your nails. Just lean against it.'

She climbed nimbly up the ladder into the branches of the apple tree. The ladder wobbled. Suze collected herself and leaned against it, hard. It stopped wobbling.

Suze tilted her head to peer up at her friend. 'What do you mean, Simon's not coming?' she demanded, outraged. 'Tonight is going to be the North London party of the year. He can't chicken out.'

Zoe set herself astride a gnarled branch and looked down. She had done this many times before and she was dressed for it: thigh-hugging cycling shorts, elderly tee shirt that didn't matter if it got torn. She had added flexible surfing shoes before coming out of the house. They improved her grip on the gnarled branches of the apple tree. Her soft brown hair was coiled round in a rough bun and skewered into place so that it did not catch on a branch. She leaned forward cautiously, holding out a hand.

'Pass me up the lights. He didn't chicken out.'

Suze handed up a worn wooden wheel. A cable of fairy lights was coiled round it like New Age barbed wire. The wheel was on a central pivot, and Zoe hooked the ends into the sling she had tied around her body for the purpose.

'Oh, don't tell me,' said Suze. 'When you returned him to store you told him he was off the guest list tonight.'

Zoe took a moment to replace a long hairpin more securely. Her wild curls never stayed in place, no matter how ruthlessly she restrained them.

'We both agreed we could do with a breathing space,' she said defensively.

'Oh, that's what it was, was it? Honestly, you're hopeless.'

Zoe clambered among leaves and twigs, uncoiling the lights. 'It seemed best,' she said in a muffled voice.

'Okay, I know you only want men on a short lease,' said Suze, unheeding. 'But you could at least have held onto Simon until after our party. That's only common sense.'

Zoe was startled into a grin. She paused and stuck her head through the leaves to look down at her friend. 'Suze Manoir, you're an exploiter of the defenceless,' she said reprovingly. 'I can't use Simon like that. It's not fair.'

Suze was unimpressed. 'Who needs to be fair? We've got three disco balls to set up.'

'We don't need a man to do that. I can put them up. No problem.'

But Zoe hesitated. She sat back, letting the leaves close around her. The afternoon sun, where it struck through the lush leaves, was sensuously hot on her skin. It was a beautiful day. It would be a perfect evening for a party.

But just now, in the hot stillness, there was no party. Just her and Suze. And Suze was her best friend. She had to tell someone the truth. It was beginning to suffocate her. If she couldn't tell Suze, who could she tell?

From her hiding place among the branches she began, 'Suze, there's something…'

But Suze did not hear. She was looking up, squinting against the sun, and laughing. 'You are so practical. You were born to be an entrepreneur.'

Zoe gave up. It was easier. You couldn't really bare your soul when one of you was sitting half-way up a tree and the other was on a pre-party high. She retreated among the foliage and carried on playing out the cable, placing the lights evenly along the very tips of branches.

And Suze did not even notice that Zoe had been on the point of sharing something. She was still contemplating the party.

'Of course you can put them up. Is there anything you can't do?'

Zoe parted the leaves again. They were greeny-gold and smelt wonderful, slightly damp and full of vegetable energy. She pushed them away from her face.

'Haven't found it yet.'

Suze shook her head. 'I can never think why I'm the one with the business career and you're still messing about temping.'

'Hair,' said Zoe calmly. 'Curly brown hair just doesn't go with a career. People don't take curls seriously. Whereas you've looked like a tycoon since you were four.'

Suze was a wide-shouldered blonde, with a habit of haughty impatience and legs to die for.

Now she sniffed. 'You could always get the hair straightened. Put in streaks, maybe.'

'I suppose so,' said Zoe, fixing lights fast.

'I'm serious Zo. It's two years since you left college. Don't you think you ought to stop messing about?'

'We're not all natural-born businesswomen,' said Zoe without rancour. 'I get by.'

'Sure, you get by. You earn your bread and you have a great life.' Suze struck the ladder with her fist to emphasise her point. 'But what about the future?'

Zoe looked down again at her, mildly surprised.

'Don't forget, I'm the one who still has a life,' she teased gently. 'When did you start to sound like your father?'

Suze gave a sharp sigh. 'I know. I know,' she said ruefully. 'Being a financial success is not all joy. Have you finished?'

'Yup. Now, if you can just stop shaking that ladder…'

'Sorry,' said Suze with a grin. 'Concentrate, Manoir. Concentrate.'

Zoe secured the last light and climbed rapidly, hand over hand, down through the branches. Clutching the trunk, she felt around for the top of the ladder with her foot. Suze reached up and directed it onto the top step.

'Thank you,' said Zoe. She slid to the ground and unhooked the wheel, with its residual cable. 'There we are. One tree dressed to welcome summer.'

'You're the business,' said Suze, admiring.

Zoe retrieved the ladder from her and retracted the extension. She clicked it back into place and hiked the ladder under her arm, turning back to the house.

'Who needs a man?' she said lightly.

Suze padded after her. 'Okay. Okay. You don't need a man to hang your party lights. What about the other stuff?'

And suddenly there it was again. Another ideal opening. *Go for it Zoe. Tell your best friend the truth.*

But she found herself prevaricating. 'What other stuff?'

Suze made a wide gesture, embracing the whole world of romance. 'Hanging together. Holidays. Giving each other breakfast in bed with the newspapers on Sunday morning.'

Zoe changed the ladder to her other side. It was quite unnecessary. The thing was not heavy. But it meant she didn't have to answer.

Not that it mattered. When Suze was into one of her 'Why You Ought to Live Like I Say' homilies, she was impossible to deflect anyway.

'I mean, with Simon you knew where you were. He's practical, too.' A thought struck her. 'And we were relying on him to pick up the booze, weren't we?'

'It's being delivered,' said Zoe hastily.

'I should have known you'd get it sorted.' Suze shook her head. 'What did he do, poor guy? Ask you to marry him?'

'Marry him? Of course not. I've only known him a couple of months.'

'Quite,' said Suze dryly. 'But men do seem to see you as settling down material. God knows why, with your record.'

The budding garden smelt of honey in the still afternoon sun. Zoe could not face spoiling it, after all. She would just have to wait for another opportunity.

She felt her coping mask twitch into place. The Zoe who could handle anything and make a joke of it, too. Privately she called it Performance Zoe.

'It's my cooking,' she said lightly. 'Ever since Gran taught me how to make bread and butter pudding I haven't been able to get men out of my hair.' She manoeuvred the ladder down a flight of four stone steps without difficulty and went to the battered garden shed. 'Can you open the door, please?'

Suze did. But, 'It's more than bread and butter pudding,' she said darkly.

Zoe disappeared inside. Various planks of the shed were rotting, and the tools were ancient, but it was painfully tidy. She hung the ladder on its allotted hook.

'I doubt it,' she said from the depths.

The house had been built on the side of a hill. As a result the garden was arranged into three wide terraces. The orchard was at the top, but this middle terrace was the largest, with a lawn and flowerbeds full of old cottage flowers. Bees buzzed among headily scented low-growing pinks. Suze flung herself down on the grass and stuffed her nose into a small grey plant with white flowers.

'Heaven,' she said dreamily. 'I suppose you do all the garden as well? No, don't answer that.'

Zoe emerged from the shed. 'What?'

Suze rolled over on her back, heedless of grass stains and creases on her expensive navy skirt. She looked up at her friend lazily. 'Come on, Zo. You know what a hot babe you are. Bread and butter pudding is just a bonus.'

Zoe sank down beside her and started plucking at the grass. 'Thank you.'

'It's true,' said Suze dispassionately. 'Men drool and women weep. If you weren't my best friend I'd have put out a contract on you by now.'

Zoe picked a daisy out of the lawn and threw it at her. 'No, you wouldn't.'

'I might. If you got your claws into one of my men.'

There was something in Suze's voice that startled Zoe. She stopped pulling at grass stalks and looked at her friend, shocked. 'I would never do that.'

'You wouldn't have to,' said Suze dispassionately. 'It must be pheromones or something. All you have to do is turn up somewhere on your own and—wham!'

'Wham?' Even Performance Zoe blinked at that. 'Get real, Suze.'

Suze sat up and linked her arms round her knees. 'It's real enough. Men—some men, anyway—take one look at you and go weak at the knees.'

'Hey, I'm not that special. I'm not even beautiful.'

'I know you're not,' her friend said candidly. 'But there's something about you.'

'Pu-lease—' said Zoe. She tried to joke but she was unnerved all the same.

'There is,' Suze insisted. 'I've seen it, again and again.' She rested her chin on her clasped knees, thoughtful. 'At first I thought it was because you didn't *try* as hard as the rest of us. I mean, your clothes were okay, but you always looked as if you'd scrambled into them at the last moment before going out. I said that to David once.'

David was Suze's boyfriend before last. Zoe had wondered several times whether Suze was as completely over him as she claimed to be. Now her voice changed and Zoe was certain.

'And David said, "Yes, exactly." That soft, rumpled look gave a man the feeling that you'd only got out of bed a few minutes ago. And that it wouldn't take too much persuasion to get you back in again.'

Zoe sat bolt upright, forgetting all about Suze's possible broken heart. 'He didn't,' she said, True Zoe taking over momentarily and genuinely appalled.

'Yup.'

'But that's—so untrue.'

'But effective,' said Suze dryly.

Zoe's nails gouged into the grass. 'It's crazy. I—'

Suze stopped hugging her knees.

'Why did you really heave Simon?' she said quietly. 'The truth, now.'

And that was the trouble, thought Zoe, scrabbling at a dandelion with real venom. Oh, she could tell Suze the truth, all right. It would only take one sentence. *He wanted to go to bed with me and I bottled out.* Only Suze would not believe her. And Zoe had no one to blame for that but herself.

There was this big fable among their friends: Zoe Brown the *femme fatale*, and the men who never lasted. Only no one knew it was a fable. Not even Suze. And Suze thought she knew everything there was to know about Zoe Brown. She very nearly did, too. Just not—

They had always told each other their secrets, from the time their mothers had walked them to kindergarten together. Suze was still telling. It was only Zoe who held back. And Suze had no idea.

Of course Zoe did not lie. Well, not exactly. She had never stood up and actually told a falsehood about any of the men she had been out with. Only people made assumptions—the men themselves did nothing to deny them—and before she knew where she was the myth of Zoe the Butterfly Lover was born. Even her brother and sister thought she changed boyfriends so often because she got bored.

Whereas the truth—

Well, it could not go on. She had sworn it at New Year, looking in the mirror in Suze's bedroom, the only stone cold sober person in the house. She had laughed and kissed poor, bewildered Alastair at miserable midnight. The smile had been plastered on her face so hard that she'd felt it would crack.

That had been when she said to herself, No more. Everyone had been talking about their shiny new resolutions. Well, that was hers. Tell Suze first. Then the rest of the world. The truth. Then she could wave goodbye to Performance Zoe for ever. And get on with the rest of her life.

Hello world, I'm a virgin.

Only she never seemed to find the opportunity. The trouble was that there was such a huge difference between what she was and what everyone—all her friends, even her brother and sister—thought she was. Even a nice man like David thought she could be persuaded to get back into bed—*back* into bed—without too much difficulty. And then, just today, here was her best friend telling her 'there's more to relationships than sex'.

Some of it was her own fault, Zoe knew. New Year was six months ago. There must have been chances to tell Suze. She had just run away from them. And, most damning of all, she had just unloaded her third escort of the year.

She said slowly, 'Okay. The truth it is. Simon's a great guy. It wasn't anything he did—'

Suze laughed wickedly. 'Okay. What was it that he *didn't* do?' And she leered with mock lasciviousness.

At once Zoe was wincing internally. But outside she was laughing back.

'Nothing to complain about. He made all the right moves. It wasn't him, honestly. It was me.'

'You don't have to tell me that. It's always you.' Suze pursed her lips. 'A complete split personality, that's what you are.'

'What?' said Zoe, arrested.

'If you ask me, you don't know what you want. You unload a swinger like Alastair because he doesn't want to play house with your barmy family. Then you hitch up with Simon who's so domestic he comes with a matching Labrador. And he can't keep you interested, either.'

Zoe shifted. 'It isn't quite like that.'

Suze was too intrigued by her own analysis to take any notice of Zoe's uncomfortable murmur.

'Don't you see a pattern? You only want what you haven't got at the moment.'

Zoe's heart sank. 'Suze, listen to me—' she began urgently.

But there was ring from the little telephone clipped to Suze's belt. She pressed a button and raised her eyebrows at the number displayed.

'Jay Christopher? What does he want?' She pressed another button and put the thing to her ear. 'Hi, Jay. What can I do for you?'

Zoe looked away across the garden. She could have kicked herself. Another ideal opportunity wasted. Again.

What is wrong with me? thought Zoe, despairing.

Meanwhile Suze had gone into crisp business mode. She even stood up to talk, prowling around the lawn as if she were patrolling her office. She snapped out questions like an interrogator, but most of the time she listened attentively.

'So that's more than a filing clerk,' she was saying when Zoe tuned in again. 'You need someone who can handle research. And work on their own initiative. And you want them by Monday. You don't ask much, do you?'

The telephone said something flattering.

Suze laughed, undeceived. 'And you know that nobody else would even think of trying. Okay, Jay, I'll do what I can. But I need the paperwork tonight and I'm not in the office. If you're serious about this, you'll have to drop it off here.' She spelled out Zoe's address.

The telephone said something else.

'Am I an online map service?' asked Suze sweetly. 'Look in the *A to Z*. The good news is it doesn't matter how late you get here. We're having a party.'

It was all the reminder that Zoe needed. She jumped to her feet. 'Time to get on,' she mouthed at Suze, and ran down the last set of steps to the patio and into the kitchen, command centre of Operation Party.

She began to attack the remaining two thirds of the big refectory table with energy.

Eventually Suze finished her phone call and followed. 'Interesting,' she said. She stood in the doorway, sucking her teeth. 'Er—Zo? About your jobs next week…'

'What?' said Zoe, scrubbing hard.

'I know you don't want to sign on with me permanently. But—what about a one-off? Two weeks, maybe four. A really stimulating job, too. Lots of initiative required, and you get to use your brain, too.'

Zoe knew her best friend well. Suze had not got to be a twenty-four-year-old phenomenon by focusing on the disadvantages of the employers who used her agency. 'What's wrong with it?'

'Nothing. Honest. It's a brilliant job.'

'Then why haven't you already got someone on your books who can do it?'

Suze sighed. 'I have. Well, a couple. But they've already got jobs for next week. And this is not a job that just anyone can do. They have to have that little bit extra.' She came and stood beside Zoe, nudging her companionably. 'Well, a lot extra, actually. You'd have been my first choice anyway.'

'You're wheedling,' said Zoe dispassionately. 'You always wheedle when there's something wrong. 'Fess up. What's the downside?'

'Well, it's in the West End,' admitted Suze.

'Uh-oh. You mean I'd have to leave the house before Harry goes to school.' She shook her head. 'No way. His exams are coming up.'

'If I can persuade them to let you arrive later? Say ten-thirty? That would mean you missed the rush hour on the tube as well.' Suze slipped an arm round her. 'Oh, come on, Zo. You know you need the money. And it'd be fun. We could have lunch together.'

Zoe hesitated. It was true; they needed the money. The plumbing had more leaks than she was able to keep up with, and a damp patch that she kept trying not to think about had appeared in the top bedroom ceiling. To have enough in her bank account to be able to call a plumber and hang the consequences sounded like heaven.

'If I could leave the house after I've seen Harry off…' she mused aloud.

'You're a sweetheart,' said Suze. She put on rubber gloves and took the scouring pad away from Zoe. 'I'll finish that.'

'I didn't say I would do it,' Zoe said hurriedly. 'I'll think about it. That's all.'

'You're a mate,' said Suze. 'That's all I ask. Thanks.'

Zoe did a rapid assessment of the contents of the fridge and shifted food around to make room for bottles of white wine.

Suze considered her thoughtfully. 'It is okay, me asking this guy tonight?'

Zoe was surprised. 'It's half your party. You ask anyone you want.'

'He's a client, but he's cool,' Suze assured her. 'In fact he's gorgeous.'

Zoe shrugged. 'Even if he isn't I can live with it. Lauren's bringing Boring Accountant Man, after all.'

They both groaned.

Suze said delicately, 'Speaking of cool—is your mum coming?'

The big house was theoretically the Brown family home. But Zoe's mother had lived a sort of semi-detached existence from her three children ever since her husband left. These days the house ran like a shared tenancy between four adults. And if anyone cooked family meals or did a major shop for the house it was Zoe, not Deborah Brown.

Zoe said without any delicacy at all, 'Not a chance. Any sign of a party and she heads for the hills.'

They were both silent, remembering. Philip Brown had walked out during Zoe's sixteenth birthday party. All the neighbours knew it. Suze's mother had been there with hot meals and a shoulder to lean on until Deborah had finally repelled her. Zoe and her siblings had been grateful for the hot meals, though. They'd stayed grateful until Zoe had taken charge and made sure that the house ran properly again.

'Shame.' Suze had gone through school envying Zoe her anti-authoritarian mother. She still had a lot of time for Deborah, though she thought the woman's withdrawal into her own world was hard on Zoe. 'She's still on Planet Potty, then?'

'Yes,' said Zoe briefly.

The doorbell rang. It was the drink for the party. Zoe and Suze helped carry in the cases. There was wine and bottled water and vodka and mixers and beer. And then four dozen wine glasses in their divided cardboard boxes.

'Sign here,' said the friendly delivery man. 'Glasses back clean by Monday. You pay for breakages. Have a good one!'

After that they were too busy for more confidences. Zoe did not know whether she was frustrated or relieved. Either way, it didn't matter.

'Help,' Zoe said as she and Suze formed themselves into a production line to unpack glasses. 'In less than three hours the house will be full of people expecting to be fed and entertained. So far only the garden is ready for them.'

But she and Suze worked well together. They were both practical and unflappable, and they had done this before. The food was set out, the drawing room disco was operational, and a bedroom full of the valuable and fragile was locked, with half an hour to spare.

Zoe showered and washed her hair quickly. She dried it fast, watching it spring into its corkscrew curls with resignation. 'Oh, well, there's nothing I can do about it. Curls are my curse.'

'Some curse.' Suze had extracted the tiniest possible slip of a dress from her briefcase. She climbed into it, then occupied Zoe's dressing table. She was peering in the mirror, outlining her eyelids carefully.

Zoe pinned her hair carelessly on top of her head and began to scrabble in her wardrobe.

'Why do I always forget how much effort it takes to organise a big party?' said Suze between clenched teeth.

'Because we're good at it.' Zoe debated between a white crop top and a black net shirt that was perfectly plain except that you could see through it. She opted for advice. 'Which do you think?'

Suze put her eye make up on hold for moment, swivelled round and considered gravely.

'Not white,' she decided. 'No tan yet.'

Zoe nodded, flung the white top back in the wardrobe and dug black satin underwear out of a drawer. Having decided, she dressed quickly, teaming the chiffon top with deep purple leather trousers, soft and clingy as gloves. Leaving Suze at the dressing table, she went into her *en suite* shower room and attacked the still damp curls with a comb. Soon they were falling into turbulent waves of gold and brown and chestnut, and even a hint of auburn.

She came out. 'What do you think?'

Suze had finished her eyes. She turned. 'Very Pre-Raphaelite,' she approved.

'Not as if I've just got out of bed?'

'Of course not.'

'So men aren't going to think I'm willing to jump right back if they ask nicely?'

Suze chuckled. 'Well, you know men. They live in hope.'

Zoe clutched her temples in mock despair.

'Never mind,' Suze consoled her. 'You can always dance with Boring Accountant Man. He doesn't back women into bed. Lauren told me he's holding out for a virgin.'

Her tone said it all, thought Zoe. He might just as well have been holding out for a tyrannosaurus rex as far as Suze was concerned.

'Really?' she said in a constrained voice.

'I don't know what Lauren sees in her weirdos. She must be on a mission to bring the twenty-first century to the unenlightened.'

Zoe bent and fluffed up her hair unnecessarily. 'I suppose so.' She sounded depressed.

Suze put an arm round her shoulders and hugged her quickly.

'Don't worry,' she said cheerfully. 'I know you're the saviour of the world's party outcasts, but Boring Accountant Man isn't going to be looking in your direction. Never seen anyone less virginal in my life.'

Zoe gave a hollow laugh. 'I'm glad about that.'

Suze chuckled. 'I don't believe there's a twenty-three-year-old virgin left in the northern hemisphere.'

Zoe winced. Only Suze did not see it, and the mask clicked into place, as it always did, without fail.

But bright, deceptive, *popular* Performance Zoe said naughtily, 'Definitely dead as a dodo.'

CHAPTER TWO

JAY CHRISTOPHER drove into the tree-lined street at half past midnight. The party house was not difficult to identify. Someone had tied balloons all along the iron railings and it blazed with lights.

He inserted the Jaguar into the tightest possible parking place with one smooth movement and switched off the engine. For a moment he sat there in the friendly dark, savouring the solitude. It had been a heavy week in every way.

'People!' he said aloud, with fierce self-mockery. 'Doncha just love them?'

He looked at the balloon-fringed house with reluctance bordering on dislike. But this was work, he reminded himself. He could deal with people when it was work.

He flicked open the slim briefcase on the passenger seat and found the big white envelope he was looking for. Then he flung the briefcase on the floor, out of sight of any potential car breaker. There was no point in bothering with a jacket. The night was too warm and he didn't think Suze Manoir's friends would welcome a fellow in a

City suit. Anyway, he had already left his tie at Carla's.

At the thought of Carla his slim dark brows locked together. She had not contributed to the emotional horrors of this week. But he knew that she was not happy. It would have to end soon, Jay thought. It could not go on, not if he was making her unhappy. No matter how bravely she denied it.

He shook his head. It was so easy to know when women were getting in too deep. They stopped asking questions in case they couldn't deal with the answers.

Take tonight, for example. He had said, without thinking, that he was going to have to drive through a part of London he did not know. That he was going to a party. Carla could so easily have asked, Whose party? Where? Could she come, too…? But she hadn't. Jay even knew why. In case he wouldn't take her. In case the party-giver was her successor.

So she had just sat opposite him in the restaurant and smiled and asked intelligent questions about his business and looked forward to seeing him on Sunday. And all the time there had been that terrible fear at the back of her eyes. And her voice had been calm and even. And she hadn't asked questions.

Yes, he was definitely going to have to end it. She was too nice a woman to do anything else. He could not let her start to hope that there might be any future for them. It would be completely false. He had made that plain when they started. Carla had said she understood that. But women had that habit of forgetting the rules when they fell in love.

Especially when they fell in love with men who did not understand love.

I might not understand love, thought Jay. But I've seen the harm it does. Oh, Carla, why can't you settle for honest sex and friendship?

But he knew she would not. His heart twisted with pity for her. Yet even as he winced at the thought of her distress he could not wait to get away. It suffocated him, all this terrible, exhausting emotion. It made him want to go out on the moors and run and run and run until he couldn't think, could barely breathe—and still keep on running.

Well, at least there would be no emotion at Suze Manoir's party. Jay laughed aloud at the thought. He got out of the car, stuffed the envelope under his arm and crossed the street.

It took him time to get into the house. Once in, though, it was relatively easy to find Suze. He tracked her down to a room with rotating disco lights and loud seventies music. She was dancing energetically to Abba, but as soon as he arrived she dropped her partner's hand and rushed across to him.

'Jay! You got here.'

'I even got in,' he said dryly. 'Who on earth have you got on the door? Murder Incorporated?'

'Oh that's Harry Brown and his friends. He's Zoe's brother.'

'Zoe?'

'She lives here. It's half her party.'

'Well, she certainly gives a great bouncer service,' he said. 'The guys out there have a technique that makes your average killer shark look like Miss Hospitality.'

'She's very efficient,' said Suze demurely. 'In fact—well, never mind. Have you got my contract?'

'Have you got my research assistant?' he countered.

'Maybe.'

She was looking naughty, he thought. Or it could be a trick of the whirling light.

He said, 'This isn't a game, Susan. I've got a major speech to give at the Communications Conference in Venice next month. And there isn't a single note or reference to build on.'

'Come and let me find you a drink,' Suze said soothingly. 'And you can tell me how you let it get away from you.'

'Something soft. I'm driving,' he said absently. 'It happened because I delegated, and the wretched girl hasn't done a thing.'

Suze opened the fridge. 'Juice or water?'

'Water, please.'

He wandered round the kitchen. The lighting was better than in the drawing room disco, but it was still clearly a room decked out for a party. There were candles and trailing greenery everywhere, and someone had sprayed 'Sixteen Again' on the mirror in gold paint.

'How old is your friend?' Jay asked, recoiling.

Suze poured water into a big wine glass for him.

'Twenty-three. But she says everyone should be sixteen at a party.'

'Original!'

Suze laughed and gave him the glass.

'She's not as daft as she sounds. She has her reasons. Now, let me have a look at that contract.'

He gave her the envelope.

'It's a long shot, I know. If you can't help, then I'll call the bigger agencies on Monday.'

Suze was running her eyes down the job description. 'Hmm? You know the other agencies aren't as creative as I am.'

'No, but they have more people on their books.'

She looked up. 'You don't want more, Jay. You want the right one. And I may just have her for you.'

He was intrigued. '*May just?* That doesn't sound like you.'

Suze grinned. 'Well, she's thinking about it. I need you to help me convince her.'

Jay sighed. 'And how do I do that?'

'Do I need to tell the great PR guru?' mocked Suze. 'Charm her. Challenge her.' She added kindly, 'You can do it!'

There was a pregnant silence. 'The bigger agencies are so much easier,' said Jay plaintively.

She laughed aloud. 'But not nearly so much fun. Now, listen, we'll need to do a double act…'

Zoe had been going upstairs when she heard the altercation at the front door. She had turned, intending to go and see if she needed to intervene. Harry and his friends could sometimes take their bouncer duties a bit too seriously, she knew.

So she had been halfway down the stairs when she saw him.

He was wearing dark trousers of some sort, and a wonderful shirt in sunset colours. Silk, she was sure. You would not have got that purity of colour in any other material. Zoe could not afford silk, but that did not stop her dreaming over it in the shops. She knew the way the material moved on the body, catching the light in a thousand different ways. As the man had stood there, arguing with Harry and his suspicious mates, she'd been almost dazzled by that sheen, that hint of gold, those little wasp stings of tangerine and apricot and purple among the principal colour.

What sort of man came to a suburban party in flame-coloured silk?

And then she'd looked at his face.

And stopped dead. Her heart had seemed to contract in her breast.

He hadn't been looking at her. He had not even seen her. If he had, he wouldn't have known her. But somehow—she knew him. She always had. Though she did not know his name.

She knew the face, though. The proud carriage of the head, like a Mogul Prince. The deep, deep eyes. The sculpted ascetic mouth, with its eloquent self-discipline and its alluring hint of passion suppressed. The energy. The fire. Banked now, certainly, but fire nonetheless. Oh, yes, she knew that face all right.

Zoe had retreated a step, backing round the corner into the shadows. She'd felt cold and very serious, as if she had just come face to face with her future.

Oh, wow! That's all I need.

It was ridiculous, of course. Nobody believed in love at first sight. It was an adolescent fantasy. A myth.

A myth like the twenty-three-year-old virgin? said a voice in her head ironically.

Well, all right, maybe it wasn't exactly a myth. Maybe it was pheromones. Maybe it was the party. They had a habit of lowering your inhibitions, parties! It was not important, anyway. It was not a feeling you could *rely* on.

It still gave you a hell of shock, thought Zoe ruefully. She felt as if she had walked into a wall.

Who on earth was he?

You don't want to know, said that voice in her head. There was a distinct warning note in it.

And it was right. Of course it was right. If she had to come face to face with the man she'd probably be as tongue-tied as a new teen with a pop idol whose poster she had had on her wall for years. That was about the level of substance to her feelings.

She did not want to have to deal with fantasies she should have outgrown ten years ago, Zoe told herself. She wanted to have a good time. That was what tonight was all about. Forget her money worries! Forget her non-existent career and her life on hold! Dance and have fun!

She would dance and have fun if it killed her, she resolved grimly.

So she had resumed her journey to her bathroom. And before she'd come downstairs again, she'd splashed water on her face so vigorously that she'd had to rebuild her make-up from scratch.

Suze took Jay back to the drawing room. Now that he'd had time to adjust, he saw it ran the depth of the house, from the street to the garden. At the far end the French windows were open to the night air. He moved towards them gratefully, picking up the rhythm of the dance as he went. Beside him Suze gyrated, a lot less rhythmically.

'She'll be here somewhere. When last seen she was listening to a man in a checked shirt talk about megabytes.'

Jay bent his head to her. 'Why?' he said simply.

'Zoe takes being a hostess seriously. She does ten minutes per no-hoper.'

Suze was twining herself round him sinuously as they walked. It would have been sexy if she hadn't been scanning the room all the time and talking nineteen to the dozen. Jay smiled at her with affection. God bless Susan, who didn't fancy the pants off him and wasn't going to break her heart over him.

'You're a star,' he said, taking her hand and dancing her powerfully through a little knot of wild arms and bouncing shoulders.

'Love it when you butter me up,' said Suze, unmoved by his touch.

They got to the windows.

'Maybe she's in the garden,' said Jay, with a longing look at the tall shadows of trees and laurel hedges.

'Maybe.' But Suze was not looking outside. He felt her jump under his hand. 'Ah, there she is.' She raised her arm above her head and waved vigorously. 'Zo! Over here!'

He looked into the shot darkness, with its shifting shadows of dancing bodies, and at first he saw nothing. Then the woman started to come towards them through the bopping crowd and he held his breath.

She was tall and graceful as a willow. As she got closer he saw she had a cloud of wild hair. He had no idea what colour. He could not tear his eyes away from her mouth. Her lips would have been voluptuous anyway, but she had painted them what looked like a dark purple. It was an aggressive colour, anyway. The whole image was aggressive. But he looked and looked, and saw vulnerability behind the image. More, there was a quivering sensitivity that their owner was trying hard to deny.

He found that he was not surprised she spent ten minutes with every no-hoper under her roof.

'Gorgeous,' he said, almost to himself.

Suze certainly didn't hear.

The woman's skin was milk-pale beneath an outrageously revealing black chiffon shirt. Under it, he could see a black bra in some shiny material. One thin strap was falling off her shoulder under the transparent sleeve. It was somehow more seductive than nakedness would have been. He felt as if he had been doused in ice water.

That graceful walk, that skin, that mouth…

Hell. Sixteen again, with a vengeance. Sixteen again, and hungry as a male animal for his conquest.

'Down boy,' said Jay grimly.

Suze had heard that, all right. 'What?' she said, startled.

'That is your candidate for my research assistant?' said Jay in disbelief.

'My friend Zoe. Yes. So?'

'Your friend?' This got worse and worse.

'Yes.' Suze faced him. 'And she really needs this job, too, though she may not want to admit it. So go carefully, right? You could be the answer to the maiden's prayer.'

Jay groaned. 'Have you even heard of political correctness?' he said. He was racked by his baser instincts. The only possible solution was to laugh. 'Maiden's prayer, for heaven's sake!'

'I'm a traditionalist,' said Suze, unmoved. She reached out an arm and hauled her friend between them. 'Zoe, this is the man you've just got to meet.'

So what's wrong with this one?

Zoe suppressed a sigh and smiled resolutely at the tall man standing next to her friend. As far as she could tell in the disco lighting he looked all right. Heck, he looked as tall as her prince from the hallway. But he had to have some mega problem or Suze would never have called her over. The party had got to the stage where you didn't make introductions.

'Hi,' she yelled, trying to make herself hear above the dance beat and only half succeeding. She fluttered her fingers at him. 'Zoe Brown.'

He did not seem to realise that that meant she had not caught *his* name. He looked bored. Dark as the devil, sleek as a seal just out of the water, and *bored*.

No-hopers didn't usually look bored. They looked sulky or wary or too eager to please. And they couldn't believe their luck when a babe like Zoe stopped by.

The tall dark man did not seem to notice that she was a babe. In fact he did not take his eyes off Suze. He looked as if he'd been sandbagged.

'Hi.' It sounded strangled.

Suze smiled and turned her shoulder on him. 'Zoe, meet your fate.'

He looked startled.

Not nearly as startled as Zoe, though. As he bent his head she realised who he was. The deep, deep eyes. If they went somewhere where the light was normal that shirt would be flame-coloured. And silk. *Definitely* not a no-hoper.

And Suze said he was *her fate*?

'What?' she said, temporarily forgetting that they would not hear her. After all, she could not hear herself. She took hold of Suze's arm and shook it hard to get her attention. 'What—did—you—say?' she mouthed with great care. Her eyes burned with indignation.

Suze's naughty smile widened.

'Nine to five for the next four weeks,' she mouthed back.

'What?'

Suze sighed visibly. She looked up at the ceiling. The rotating light balls, hired for the party, were making a great success of turning the Edwardian mouldings into a starship re-entry burst. She shrugged and waved them both to the

French windows, with great traffic policeman gestures.

There were no speakers in the garden, at least. Between the incessant beat and the noise of the party it was not exactly silent, but at least you could hear what people were saying. Not that most people came out here to talk. There were several couples, dancing or lying on the grass, heads close, not talking.

Out in the dark, where no one could see, Zoe flinched. Performance Zoe took her to task. *So what else is new?* No point in minding. That's what people do at parties.

She even did it herself sometimes. Only she just did it for the look of the thing. Then sidled out later, when she could. Not that anyone noticed her sidling out. If anyone were to suggest that popular Zoe Brown had never gone beyond a kiss in the dark, her friends would split their sides.

She did not want them splitting their sides tonight. Not in front of the Mogul Prince. Performance Zoe took control.

''Scuse me,' said Zoe, shimmying past a couple gazing fixedly into each other's eyes and shifting from foot to foot in a rhythm that was at least three tracks ago.

She made for the orchard terrace, pounding up the uneven York stone steps with the surefootedness of long practice. The others followed.

Zoe turned, hands on her hips, ready for confrontation.

The smooth-as-a-seal man was already on to it, though. He had obviously decided to stop being bored. Suze was beginning to look alarmed.

Suze's father was a judge. Nobody ever alarmed Suze.

The man said with dangerous quietness, 'Want to explain, Susan?'

Well, it sounded dangerous to Zoe. In fact the hair came up on the back of her neck at the deep drawl.

'Er…' said Suze, floundering.

She never floundered, either. She was as quick on her feet as Zoe. In fact Zoe had learned her 'Evasive Manoeuvres For When the Conversation Gets out of Hand' from Suze in the first place. And Zoe was the best.

'I've been conned, haven't I?' said the tall dark man in a level voice. 'I want a professional job. And you think you can unload one of your ditzy friends.' His eyes skimmed Zoe briefly. 'No offence.'

'Ditzy friend?' she gasped.

Suze sent her an exasperated look before returning to her main opponent. 'Chill out, Jay. I'm doing my best—'

'I need someone to *work*,' he said intensely. 'Not a filing clerk in a micro skirt.'

'Zoe can hack it.' Suze waved a hand. 'Zoe can do anything.'

The man swung round on Zoe and she swallowed hard. In the flickering light of the summer candles he looked about ten feet tall.

Ten feet tall and mad as a hornet was not the ideal prospective employer. *Thank you, Suze.*

She said furiously, 'I never agreed—'

He raised his eyebrows. 'Nor did I. A research assistant able to work on her own initiative?' he asked pleasantly, not taking his eyes off Zoe. 'I don't think so.'

Zoe stiffened. 'I beg—your—pardon?'

'I know what she can do,' snapped Suze. 'Zoe and I used to go to school together.'

His eyes were unreadable in the dark, but his whole stance said he didn't believe a word of it.

'Oh, yes? And when did St Bluestocking's start turning out unskilled filing clerks?'

Zoe flinched all over again.

Plenty of people thought she was wasting her university education by doing temporary jobs in a variety of offices. Only last week her father had taken her out to lunch and tried to probe, delicately, when she was going to get a real job. But no one had actually told her to her face that she was unskilled. Or implied that she was a thing of no worth because of it.

She forgot the passionate mouth and the mogul silk. She decided he was all ten feet tall hornet man. And she hated him.

She said clearly, 'I'm temping while I consider my options.'

It was true, too. Only—she had been considering her options for two years now and was no nearer finding a solution. She was not going to admit that to hornet man, though.

He looked her up and down. She could not see his face but she could *feel* the hard, swift appraisal. He took a couple of step towards her, lithe as a panther padding around its prey, assessing whether it was worth the effort of the chase or not.

Not that he could see much in the candlelit dark. Maybe her long, soft hair as it waved loosely about her shoulders in the night breeze. Or the glittery black see-through stuff of the shirt that left her shoulders visible and her slim midriff exposed. Enough to realise that she looked as cool as Suze, anyway.

And that, of course, was the trouble. She looked as cool and confident as any other girl here. More confident than most, maybe, especially when she was wearing these soft glove-leather trousers that hugged her slim hips and turned Suze green with envy.

She *looked* just fine. It was only inside that she knew she wasn't. Wasn't confident. Wasn't fine. Wasn't *normal*.

And wasn't going to admit to any of it. Well, not in front of hornet man. She stuck her chin in the air and glared at him. And took a decision.

'You can stop looking me up and down as if I'm livestock. You get my time nine to five, starting Monday morning,' she told him crisply. 'And that's all your money buys you. Friday nights aren't in the package.'

Suze drew in an audible breath.

He was taken aback. His head went back as if she had driven a foil straight at his chest.

Then he said dryly, 'That sounds like St Bluestocking's, all right.'

Zoe was still angry. 'So apologise.'

Suze gave a soft whistle. But the man said slowly, 'For what?'

'For looking at me like that.'

'Aren't you being a bit over-sensitive?' He was amused.

Amused! Zoe decided she wanted blood.

'If I am, then you won't want me to work for you, will you?' she said with shining amiability.

'I never said—'

She shook her head. 'You know what over-sensitive people are like,' she told him earnestly. 'A real strain. Especially if management isn't geared up to cope. So disruptive in a small office. *Much* better if we just call it quits now.'

And just see if Suze can get you someone else by Monday morning, you jerk.

She thought he would backtrack fast. But he didn't. He looked at her for a long moment. In quite a different way this time.

Then he said, 'What makes you think that the office is small?'

Zoe gave a rather good start of surprise. 'Isn't it?' she asked, all artless confusion. 'I just thought if they let someone like you hire the staff they wouldn't be big enough to afford a proper human resources manager.'

Suze sucked on her teeth audibly.

But the man did not say anything for a moment. Then, 'I—see. Yes, I can follow your reasoning there.' His voice was tinged with unholy amusement.

For some reason Zoe suspected he had scored a point there, though she could not quite see what it was.

She said, 'I really don't think I should take the job if you're not sure about my temperament…'

He laughed aloud. 'I think you'll cope.'

'Oh, but I wouldn't want you to be uncomfortable—'

'Yes, you would,' he interrupted. 'And I don't blame you, either.'

That disconcerted her. 'Is that an apology?' she said suspiciously.

'I suppose it is.' He sounded surprised at himself. He swung round on Suze, a silent spectator for once. 'I apologise to both of you. I shouldn't leap to conclusions. Sorry, Susan.' He made her an odd, formal little bow, then looked at Zoe. 'And sorry Ms Bluestocking, too. I'll see you on Monday morning. No more snide remarks, Scout's honour.'

'Thank you,' said Zoe. She meant to sound dignified, but even to her own ears it came out just plain sulky.

Suze sent her a quick, worried look. Hornet man did not notice.

'That's settled, then,' he said cheerfully. 'So now I'll be on my way.'

Suze didn't like that. 'Going on to another party, Jay?'

He laughed. 'Weekend in the country. And I'm not going to get there until after three in the morning at this rate. I'm not going to be popular.'

'She'll wait up for you,' said Suze dryly.

But she did not say it very loudly, and Jay Whoever-he-was, running lightly down the steps and back among the partygoers, did not seem to hear.

Zoe let out a long, shaky breath and leaned against the trunk of the apple tree. Her legs felt as if they were made of cotton wool. Gently vibrating cotton wool.

'Tell me it's not true,' she begged. 'Tell me I haven't just signed up with Captain Blood!'

Suze was watching the slim dark figure find his sure-footed way down the terraces and disappear into the house. 'Captain Blood?' she echoed absently.

'He looked me up and down as if I was in a corsair slave market.'

Suze jumped and re-engaged attention. 'You watch too many old movies. Jay Christopher is no pirate.'

'Then why does he prowl like one?'

Suze gave an incredulous laugh. 'He doesn't. You're just saying that because you fancy him.'

Zoe jumped as if her friend had turned the garden hose on her. 'You've got to be joking. Why would I fancy him?'

'Everyone does,' said Suze simply.

'Can't imagine why,' Zoe muttered.

'Get real, Zo. You saw the man. He's lethal.'

'He's rude and arrogant.'

'He can afford to be arrogant. You didn't seem to clock it, but that was the man himself. Jay Christopher of Culp and Christopher Public Relations.' There was a faint question mark in Suze's voice.

Zoe pushed her hair back. 'So?'

'The Big Cheese. The one the financial reporters write the big profiles of.'

Zoe refused to be impressed. 'You know me. I don't read the financial pages.'

'He hangs out in the sports section as well. To say nothing of the gossip columns. Olympic medallist. One of the long-distance races. You must remember him.'

But Zoe shook her head. 'You know me. No competitive edge.'

Suze almost danced with frustration. 'You *must* remember. No one rated him. And then he just came from nowhere and took the medal.'

A chord in Zoe's memory started to vibrate very gently. She had a vague picture of an old television news bulletin—a tall, proud figure with remote eyes, in spite of his heaving chest and sweat soaked running gear.

Well, the eyes were right. Though that flame-coloured silk suggested that he had not broken out into a sweat in long while.

'Maybe I do remember,' she said.

'He set up his public relations agency with Theodora Culp, the business journalist. Now it's one of the best in London. Theodora's gone back into television, of course, so Jay runs it single-handed.' Suze laughed. 'And you thought he was a human resources manager.'

'I told him he was a *bad* human resources manager,' Zoe reminded her. For some reason it felt like a small triumph. Because she had been fighting back, she supposed, not melting into a warm puddle of sub-teen lust at his feet. She would have died rather than admit it, but Suze was not the only one who fancied Jay Christopher.

'He won't care. Jay's not mean. And he knows how good he is.' Suze was thoughtful for a moment. 'They say one of the big international advertising agencies is sniffing round Culp and Christopher at the moment. If Jay sells out he'll be making himself some serious money.'

But if Zoe was unwillingly attracted to the tall man with the remote eyes, she did not give a hoot about serious money. She did not have to say so. Her expression said it all.

'You've got to admire him,' Suze urged. 'He did it all on his own. His grandfather's a brigadier, and terribly well connected. But Jay wouldn't let him help out, even when the business was just two men and a dog to begin with. Jay would have every right to be insufferably pleased with himself. But he isn't.'

'No?' Zoe was sceptical.

'Well, not normally. You did seem to rub him up the wrong way.'

Zoe bristled. 'It's mutual.'

'I could see that. Never seen a man wind you up so fast in my life. And plenty have tried. You're always Miss I Can Cope.'

If only you knew.

But she didn't say that. *Why* didn't she say that? She wanted to get rid of this false image that her best friend had of her, didn't she? So why the heck did she flick back her hair, strike an attitude and go into the performance Suze expected?

'I still am. I got that man to apologise.' She even *sounded* complacent.

Megabyte Man would say I need a hard drive diagnostic.

'Yes. I suppose it's all right.' Suze sounded doubtful.

'It will be fine,' Performance Zoe said breezily. 'I've worked for some stinkers in my time. Now I've broken his resistance Mr Successful will be a piece of cake.'

Suze just looked at her.

Zoe's chin came up another ten degrees. 'So?' she challenged. 'You don't really think I can't handle him? Do you? *Me?*'

Suze put her head on one side. 'How long have we been friends?'

'Nineteen years,' said Zoe, literally.

'Then believe me. You really, really can't handle Jay Christopher.'

Performance Zoe snorted. She had a wide repertoire of dismissive noises.

'I know you. I know Jay Christopher.' Suze shook her head wisely. 'Take my advice. You don't want to go there.'

'And why not?'

'Don't forget—I know all your ex-boyfriends, Zo.'

Even Performance Zoe was silenced.

Suze shook off her unaccustomed seriousness. 'Come on. The night is young. We've got some serious partying to get in before dawn.'

She was not wrong. And Zoe was the life and soul of it. She danced with Megabyte Man, and Lauren's boring accountant, and Alastair, whom she had made miserable five months ago, and who now had a brilliant French girlfriend. She danced on her own. She draped her arms over the shoulders of her sister Artemis and Suze and did an untidy high-kicking routine.

As the sky began to lighten only the long-distance party animals were still there.

'Come on,' said Zoe, finding a fast song about a rodeo cowboy. 'Line-dance.'

They lined up and went into the rapid routine that they had worked out last Christmas. Amid raucous insults and much giggling, they managed to keep up for a bit. But in the end too many of them went right while the others went left. Finally

Harry did a sideways jump into Suze and the whole line staggered. The music raced away from them. They ended up in heap on the floor, laughing.

'Great party,' said the stragglers, tumbling out into the grey morning.

By morning, though, there were only six people left in the shabby kitchen. Hermann, who was Suze's current favourite, sat on the corner of the scrubbed pine table, plucking at a guitar and singing softly. He was waiting for Suze to take him home to bed and everyone knew it.

Zoe's younger sister, Artemis, clutched her boyfriend sleepily round the waist as he systematically loaded empty bottles into a cardboard box. From time to time Ed put an absent hand behind his back and patted her hip encouragingly.

Suze and Zoe had bagged up all the food remains in three black sacks and were now loading the dishwasher with the last of the glasses.

This was after Suze had taken Harry on one side and briefed him tersely about his sister's imminent employment prospects.

'She really needs this job,' she ended fiercely.

Harry might be only seventeen but he was a realist. He nodded slowly.

'Yup. And not just for the money. She needs to do something for herself. And something to stop Mum thinking she only has to call and Zoe will be there. Okay, Suze. Leave it to me.'

Thereafter Harry wandered among the debris, theoretically helping. In practice he was eating any food that he decided there was no room in the fridge for.

'You'll be sick,' said Zoe, matter-of-factly.

Harry grinned. 'I'm seventeen. My digestion is at peak performance.'

'It was our best party ever,' said Suze with satisfaction. 'Did you get to see Jay, Hermann? Hermann was at college with Jay,' she explained to Zoe. 'That's how I got a nibble at the Culp and Christopher account in the first place.'

'I saw him.' Suze's boyfriend executed a rippling final chord and put the guitar away. 'Nice of him to come.'

'Why shouldn't he?' demanded Suze, bridling.

Hermann was peaceful. 'He's running with the great and the good these days. Not a lot of time for simple socialising.'

Zoe sniffed. She was not surprised, somehow. The Mogul Prince had that look of a man who could hardly bring himself to bother with other people.

'Don't scare Zoe,' Suze warned. 'She's going to work for him on Monday.'

'I'm not scared. I was not intending to make friends with the man,' Zoe said crisply.

Artemis's Ed laughed. 'You can't scare Zoe. One flash of those big brown eyes and men just roll over with their paws in the air—don't they Zo?'

Artemis rubbed her cheek against Ed's bent back. 'Are you going to be long, lover? I'm wiped.'

Zoe was irritated. 'Like Suze was telling me earlier, there's more to human relationships than sex, Edward.'

There was burst of ribald laughter from the other five.

'That's a good one, coming from you, sis,' said Artemis fondly. 'The last of the *femmes fatales*.'

For once Performance Zoe did not flip into action automatically. Maybe because she was tired.

'Don't be ridiculous,' she snapped.

She seized a damp cloth and worked vigorously at the stains on the table where Ed's wine bottles had stood.

Artemis unwound herself from Ed's hips. 'Oh, come on, Zo. You know it's true. Your men hardly ever get beyond the fourth date. And I know that they call you and call you because I take the messages. So if it's not them getting bored, what is it? Picky, picky Princess Zoe, that's what.'

Zoe bit her lip. If they knew the truth they wouldn't laugh like this. On the other hand she had worked quite hard so that they *wouldn't* know the truth.

And Ed's next remark proved how right she had been to do so.

'Hey, don't worry, babe,' he said, straightening with the box of bottles in his arms. 'I think it's cool.' He flourished the box at Zoe in a sort of elephantine salute. 'My friend the heartbreaker. Ta-da.'

'Could solve your career problems,' suggested Suze. 'See if MI5 has an opening for Olga the Beautiful Spy.'

Zoe threw the cloth at her.

And everyone laughed. Just as they always did.

Zoe poured detergent, slammed the dishwasher shut, selected a program and switched it on. Everyone stood up with relief.

'Thanks for the help with the clearing up, guys. I love you tonight, but I'll really worship you tomorrow,' Zoe said. 'Hermann—take her home. She's out on her feet.'

'Little mother of all the world,' teased Suze.

But Suze was drooping, and everyone knew it. Hermann packed his guitar away in its case and put his arm round her.

'Lean on me, babe.'

Zoe looked away. Nobody noticed.

'All of three doors down the street,' scoffed Suze.

But she leaned into him gratefully and they wrapped their arms round each other. They were muzzy with sleep and low-grade lust. But they looked back to wave as they wandered off into the clear morning.

'Goodbye,' said Artemis and Ed, plodding off in the direction of his flat over the paper shop, leaning into each other and swinging their clasped hands. Artemis slept at Ed's at the weekends. Well, more like all the time now.

Harry wandered off to his room with a video and a paper plate of garlic bread.

Zoe decided she was too alert to go to bed. She made herself some hot chocolate. Hot chocolate was Zoe's long-term comfort drink. She had been brewing a lot of it lately.

She poured it into the heavy dragon-adorned mug her father had brought back from a trip. He had given it to her just before he'd told her he was moving out. It used to be a family joke: she got the things with dragons on them; Artemis had cats; Harry had crocodiles. No one had given Zoe anything with dragons on it since that day. She was glad.

She would have been quite glad if the dragon mug had been broken, but somehow it was too sturdy. Other mugs came into the house and got pushed off tables or dropped on the stone patio or trodden to dust when someone left them on the carpet after watching television. But solid old dragon just kept on going.

Seven years now. She had been sixteen then. That was why her parties always said, 'Sixteen Again'. At sixteen she had turned into—what was it Suze called her? Little mother of all the world. Yes, that was it. At sixteen Zoe had turned into the household's Responsible Adult. And she still was.

At least the thick dragons kept the drink warm. That was useful. The dawn had a chill to it.

Zoe went out onto the patio and sat down on the worn old bench. She held the mug under her chin, brooding.

Artemis was right when she said that Zoe never let a man take her out more than four times. Sometimes she did not let them take her out twice. They looked at her, saw her long legs and fashionably slim figure. They listened to her and heard a sharp tongue and a cool party girl with loads of friends. And nobody—*nobody*—saw that it was an act.

Responsible adult. Hot babe. Cool gal. The last virgin in the northern hemisphere.

'What a mess,' said Zoe wryly. She shivered, in spite of the hot drink between her hands.

Miss I Can Cope. That was what Suze had called her. She believed it, too. Zoe was not sure how. She knew that her family saw what they wanted to see. But how could her best friend be fooled?

Because you're good at the performance.

Well, good enough. Up to a point. One day soon someone was going to find her out. She felt the chill touch her again. Maybe she had met him now.

She had so nearly given herself away tonight, with the way she had stared at the Mogul Prince. He had seen it, too. She knew he had. He had looked at her so hard that she'd thought he was going to be able to draw her. And his face had told her absolutely nothing.

Had he seen through her act? Had he?

No, she told herself. Of course he hadn't. It had just been a trick of the disco ball lighting. And her own uneasy conscience, of course.

Heck, at one point it had even sounded as if he and Suze were play-acting. How was that for paranoia?

You've got to do something about that, she said to herself, as she had done so many times before. Stop performing. *Tell* someone.

But who? And how? And would they believe her, anyway?

The men in her life took their cue from her friends. And her friends knew that she was a sophisticated twenty-three-year-old with a cool life and a hot wardrobe. They even asked her advice about their love lives, for heaven's sake. And Suze was forever asking her to look out for any social incompetents who turned up at her parties. Because Zoe knew all there was to know about men and the dating game. Didn't she?

Not one of her friends would believe that twenty-year-old Artemis knew more about love than Zoe did. Heck, seventeen-year-old Harry probably knew more. And one day soon, if she did not tell them, she was going to trip up spectacularly over her half-lies and evasions.

Or she was going to get stuck in the performance. And she would be performing for the rest of her life. And *not one* soul would know her. Ever.

'Aaaargh,' she said aloud. And dashed the dragon mug on the weedy paved slabs.

It did not break.

CHAPTER THREE

JAY let himself out of the kitchen door, as he always did for his morning run. The old manor house felt asleep. He did some stretches, looking at the way the early-morning sun turned the Cotswold stone to the colour of warm butter. He smiled. His grandfather's house smiled back at him.

He stopped stretching and started off on the familiar route, his trainers picking up damp from the dew-wet grass.

Across the kitchen garden. Through the iron gate in the wall and into the woods. Along the grassy track that followed the stream back up the hill. It was easy, this first part of the course, a gentle slope and an even surface to run on. He found his pace and let his thoughts wander.

It had been an easy journey last night. The roads had been nearly empty. He had been in bed just after two. That was not so different from the hours he kept in London. Lethal if he were in serious training, of course. Only he wasn't. It was a long time since he had competed, except in the boardroom.

A long time since I have had to try at anything.

Except he had had to try last night. Suze had been right. He had been surprised to find that the girl with the voluptuous mouth was so hostile to working for him.

No, he corrected himself, she was hostile to working for Culp and Christopher. She did not know *him.* At least, he hoped it was Culp and Christopher.

Anyway, he had followed Suze's advice. He had challenged her. And before she knew where she was, she was promising to turn up on Monday morning and make him eat his words. That had made him feel as if he had won a victory.

Careful, he told himself wryly. You don't want a resurgence of the old male animal. Not at work. Not after last time.

But the thought of Zoe Brown making him eat his words set his feet pounding faster all the same.

He had to make a conscious effort to slow down. On a three-hour-run you did not start off by sprinting. And Jay was a patient man. He was good at biding his time. Even better at self-control.

He remembered the way her satin bra strap had slipped under that damned transparent shirt and he had to remind himself fiercely that self-control was his strongest point.

And you don't pursue women who work for you either, he added.

But she's only temporary. After a week or two she won't be working for me. And by then she won't be hostile any more. I'll make certain of that.

He was back by nine-thirty. He changed rapidly and went into the breakfast room. His grandfather was there, eating grilled kidneys and fulminating over the newspaper.

'Good morning. Been for a run?'

'Yes.'

'What was your time?'

Jay's hair was still damp from the shower. He pushed his fingers through it. 'Not what it should be,' he said ruefully. 'I'm getting fat and lazy in London.'

His grandfather pursed his lips. 'No, you're not. But you're not enjoying yourself much, either. Are you?'

Jay was startled. 'Aren't I?'

His grandfather rattled the *Daily Telegraph* at him. 'It says here you're going to sell out to Karlsson.'

Jay poured himself juice. 'The word is merge, Gramps. They'd do the advertising. We'd do the PR. We'd share the research. There are lots of synergies.'

'Except they're a bunch of international sharks and you're an honourable man,' said his grandfather.

Jay shrugged. 'Can't stand in the way of progress,' he said lightly.

'You ought to compete again,' said his grandfather. 'You're not too old. Cross-country running is a mature man's sport.'

Jay's lips twitched. 'Thank you. I'm thirty-five, not ninety.'

'Better use of your time than making more and more money you don't need,' said his grandfather. 'It's time you—'

'—settled down,' said Jay, his mouth suddenly grim. 'So you've said before. Thank you for your advice.'

'I only—'

Jay put down his juice and leaned forward. 'No.'

'What?'

'No,' said Jay again, very quietly.

His grandfather had commanded men and negotiated with leaders, foreign and domestic, who had volatile temperaments and the means to enforce their will. He had never been silenced by anyone as he was by his grandson. He huffed a bit. But he did not say any more.

Before dinner that night, though, he said to his daughter-in-law, 'I—er—mentioned the future this morning.'

Bharati Christopher looked at him with calm eyes. She had iron-grey hair and her son's air of detachment.

'That will only drive him away.'

'But—'

'He will marry when he falls in love. Not before.' She added, very deliberately, 'He is like his father in that.'

Brigadier Christopher had thrown his son out long before Robert went on the hippy trail to India and met Bharati. But the old man never forgot that he had missed the first seven years of his grandson's life because he had stubbornly refused to admit that a cross-cultural union had ever taken place.

Now his eyes fell.

He harrumphed. 'I suppose Jay will go off to see that gardening trollop tomorrow.'

Her eyes lit with affectionate laughter. They had mended their fences a long time ago. 'Or tonight, if you start telling him how to run his life.'

But Brigadier Christopher had the last word.

'Not my Jay. He doesn't spend the night. Taught him that myself. Spend the whole night with a woman and she gets serious. Jay,' he said with satisfaction, 'knows how to keep his affairs under control.'

Zoe zipped through the rest of the clearing up in a couple of hours on Saturday morning. She liberated the family's few decent pieces of furniture from their locked sanctuary in her mother's room. By lunchtime the house was back to normal.

'When's Mother coming back?' said Harry, appearing heavy-eyed at two in the afternoon.

Zoe was stretched out on her stomach on the sunlit lawn, reading a novel. She squinted up at him.

'When Aunt Liz kicks her out, I guess.'

He flopped down beside her. 'I hope she stays away until the mocks are over,' he said, surprising her.

She sat up. 'Really?'

'She makes me jumpy.'

Zoe pulled a face. 'She only wants you to do well.

'When she remembers,' he said with brutal truth 'Then she tries to cram a year's worth of nagging into three days.'

Zoe gave a choke of laughter. 'Do you want me to change the locks?'

'No, but—don't persuade her to come back if she wants to stay with Aunt Liz,' he said in a rush.

'Harry—are you really worried about these exams?' she asked seriously.

'No.' He was matter-of-fact. 'I've done the work and I've got the brain. But everyone at school is going a bit mad. I need to stay focused and not get in a flap. And mother flaps me.'

She thought about that. 'You mean minimal fuss, right?'

'Yes.'

'So if I get a job which means I have to leave the house before you go off to school in the morning, that wouldn't bother you?'

He was surprised. ''Course not.'

'So what do you want to make these next few weeks least stressful?'

'Regular meals and no one crowding me,' said Harry promptly.

It was like being let off a major task. Zoe laughed and ruffled his hair.

'You've got it.'

And she would be at Culp and Christopher so early she would make the Mogul Prince's eyes spin in his head, she promised herself. This summer was going to be *fun*.

Jay Christopher snapped awake as he always did, instantly alert. He was alone in the mussed Sunday-afternoon bed. Surprised, he came up on one elbow, looking round.

The room was full of dusty sunshine, but the shadows were longer than he'd expected. The summer afternoon was hot and very still. There was not so much as a tweet from the birds in the tall trees outside, although all the windows were open to the air.

The woman was standing at the open French window. She had thrown a blue kimono over her nakedness. He had brought it back from Japan for her at Christmas. They had only just started seeing each other then. She had been delighted, dancing round the room, laughing.

She was not dancing now. She turned and stood there, watching him levelly.

Jay's heart sank. Here we go again, he thought. *Why are you like this? Are you commitment-phobic? What do I have to do to make you love me?*

He looked at his watch. It was the only thing he was wearing.

'Time I was on my way back.'

The woman's eyes flickered. He braced himself.

But all she did was pull the kimono round her and say quietly, 'Yes, of course.'

He drew a sigh of relief. He liked Carla. He never told her lies. He had been faithful ever since they'd got together. And he was always honest about how little he was committed; how far he was from being able to commit.

She had always said that was enough. But lately it had not seemed enough any more. Some of their recent goodbyes had been positively scratchy. He had been here before. It was beginning to look as if it was time to move on.

Jay knew himself very well. He was not going to change. And Carla was too nice to hurt. The last couple of times he had left she had had that taut, holding-in look that he dreaded seeing on a woman's face. He knew it meant they were being brave, and he hated it.

But now she went and sat on the dressing stool and brushed her dark hair, chatting cheerfully through the bathroom door while he showered.

'Heavy week?'

'The usual.' Jay rootled through the bathroom cupboard for unscented shampoo. Ever since Carla had found that he did not like to use her lavender-scented stuff she had stocked up on an alternative. 'At least I've got rid of the troublemaker. New girl starts on Monday.'

He turned on the shower and got under it.

Carla knew about the troublemaker. She had even held hands with him fondly, all through an office party, hoping that it would discourage the girl's patent crush before any harm was done. It had not worked, but they had been friends then, united in their kindly conspiracy.

'Was it difficult?'

Jay soaped his hair viciously. 'She cried.'

'Poor Jay. That's bad.'

'You're laughing at me,' he said, pleased.

But her voice was odd. 'No. I'm laughing at me.'

He did not like the sound of that. He rinsed off his hair, the brief flare of hope dying. He stuck his head out of the bathroom door and she passed him his discarded underwear.

'Thanks.'

She carried on talking as he towelled off. 'Travelling?'

'Not too bad, for once. Brussels on Wednesday, but I'm hoping I can get in and out in a day. Manchester, and then a couple of question marks.'

She laughed. 'It sounds so glamorous. But I've done it. I know it's all cramped planes and wasting time in dirty airports.'

'Wasting a lot less time since they invented laptops.'

'Do you ever want to stop?' she asked curiously.

Jay curbed a sigh. Here it comes, he thought. He could write the script.

Don't you ever get tired of your frenetic lifestyle? Wouldn't it be nice to stay in the same place for a while? We could put a home together. Share our lives.

He said quietly, 'No, I don't ever want to stop.'

He came out of the shower room in his underpants. Towelling the sleek dark hair, he looked at her.

He said gently, 'I'm a migratory animal, Carla. You always knew that.'

She looked away. 'Yes, but—'

He did not want her to hurt herself any more by making a case that he knew was hopeless. 'I've done the country house bit,' he said firmly, pulling on dark chinos. 'Along with the neighbours in for drinks at Christmas and the ten-year plan for the garden. I was brought up with it. That's how I know it isn't me.'

The country cottage, with its fruit trees and summer-silent birds, was hers. She was a gardener by training, a journalist and broadcaster by profession. But he was beginning to see that she was a home-maker by instinct. Only it would never be his home. He saw the moment when she accepted it.

'Yes, I see,' she said after a long pause. She stood up.

Jay braced himself. But she was only getting the fine silk shirt from where he had hung it on the wardrobe handle.

'Nice colour,' she said.

He knew she didn't mean it. Carla was a successful, professional woman. She liked her men in conservative suits. In Carla's world, real men wore crisp white shirts in town, earth colours in the country. She had never come to terms with Jay's taste for hot ochre and tangerine and emerald.

Today it was turquoise. His grandfather—his lost grandfather, soft-voiced and laughing in the endless dusty enchantment of Jay's childhood—would have said that it was the colour of hopeful travel. Jay thought of it as that shade of the sea where it meets the sky: the horizon on a clear day with calm water. Carla would not have got on with his lost grandfather.

'I like it,' he said truthfully.

Carla shrugged, as she always did when they disagreed. For a moment he wondered if things would be better if they argued. But he knew, in his heart of hearts, that they wouldn't. He was a man born to be alone. He could not change that, no matter what Carla did.

She made a brave effort at a smile. 'Is the new girl nice? Or don't you know yet?'

Jay grinned. 'I know. She's a slick chick with her life under control. Gives great parties. Also I insulted her, and she hates my guts.'

'Good grief. Is that going to make for a good working relationship?'

He laughed aloud. 'Well, at least she's not going to fall in love with me,' he said with feeling. 'Couldn't take that again.'

He regretted it at once. Only, of course, once you've said it, you can't call it back. She looked stricken.

He had meant that he couldn't take another puppyish filing clerk with her eyes following him all round the office and her passionate ill-spelled e-mails. But that was not what Carla had heard. And maybe that was not all he had meant, after all.

'Hell, I'm sorry.'

'Don't worry about it.'

He slipped his arms into the shirtsleeves and shook out the silk. For a moment the turquoise stuff billowed around his golden chest like a parachute settling. He glimpsed it over her shoulder in the mirror. The silk shimmered, like the cloak of one of the Mogul emperor's bodyguards that his grandfather had shown him in old paintings. Not his lost grandfather. The other one, the Brigadier, with his impeccable standards and his careful culture and the sherry on Boxing Day. Carla got on just fine with the Brigadier.

He buttoned the shirt briskly. Ran fingers through his still-damp hair. Looked at his watch again.

'I know,' she said dryly. 'You have to go or you'll run into the Sunday evening traffic.'

'You're an understanding woman,' he teased.

'Yes.' But she did not laugh.

She came down the rickety stairs with him, still in the kimono. She did not let it billow. She clutched it round her like a blanket in a storm. At the front door she put a hand on his arm as he went to slip the latch.

'Jay—'

He suppressed irritation. He had so nearly got out of the door without a fight! But he was a gentleman. Both grandfathers had seen to that, in their different ways. He turned to her courteously.

'Yes, my dear?'

She gave a faint smile. 'Thank you, Jay.'

'What?' He was bewildered.

'You have such lovely manners. But I'm not your dear. And it's time we both faced it.'

He searched her face. She was rather pale, but her eyes were steady. No pleas, no desperation. Jay had never respected her more.

'Is it?' he said gravely.

She swallowed, but then she nodded once, decisively. 'I made myself a promise. If you looked at your watch as soon as you woke up today I'd finish it. You did. So I am.'

He winced. 'I'm sorry.'

'Don't be. It's overdue.'

'I mean I'm sorry I hurt you,' Jay said painfully.

She shook her head. 'It's a shame. I could have loved you if— But you don't let anyone get close. Maybe you're right and you can't. Well, not me, anyway. Time I recognised that.'

He had nothing to say.

She bit her lip. 'I've met someone. It's nothing yet. But—it might be, in time. If you know what I mean.'

'Yes,' he said heavily. 'I know what you mean.'

Carla's chin came up. 'I don't want to cheat. Not on you. Not on him. Not on myself. So—I want to be free now. Free to look for a relationship that works for me.'

Jay drew a long breath. 'Can we be friends?'

'Maybe. I don't want to see you for a bit, though.'

He was surprised at how much it hurt. But he had no right to complain. Carla had never lied, either. This sort of rejection came with the way he ran his life. From the way he was.

'Very well.' He touched her face briefly. 'Call me when I can buy you a drink.'

She gave him a watery smile. 'Sure.'

On a burst of anger at himself he said, 'I wish—'

But she stopped him, soft fingers over his mouth. 'No, you don't. You know yourself very well, Jay Christopher. You don't have to tell white lies to comfort me.'

'No. I know I don't.' He kissed her quickly on the mouth. They had been making love just a couple of hours ago, but already it felt awkward, as if she were a stranger. 'I hope you find what you're looking for.'

She brushed back his hair. 'You, too. You'd be a prince—if anyone could ever get through.'

She closed the door before he reached the garden gate.

It was lonely journey back. He liked lonely.

He played sitar music. And Josquin des Pres. And Bach. Every girlfriend he had ever had hated them all. It was exhilarating, playing them again, not having to tread carefully any more.

But not as exhilarating as it had once been. He had hurt Carla. He had never meant to. He had tried not to. She had said she understood his limitations, accepted them. But in the end he had hurt her. It didn't feel good.

Was it always going to be like this?

You'd better give up nice women, he told himself bitterly. You can't change. And they can't cope.

But what was the alternative? One-night stands? He pulled a face.

His lost grandfather had said to him once, 'You must be careful. Very few men are made for solitude.'

But, as Carla had said, Jay Christopher knew himself very well. And he knew that he needed the right to walk away from a relationship—any relationship—the way he needed the right to breathe.

'Hello, solitude,' he said aloud. 'Welcome back.'

CHAPTER FOUR

DEBORAH BROWN came back on Sunday afternoon. She walked out into the garden, where Artemis and Ed were playing a deeply dishonest game of croquet and Zoe was swinging in a hammock, and it was as if the sun had gone in.

'What are you *doing*?' said Deborah, in a high, anxious, scolding voice. 'Harry should be studying. Zoe, you know how important it is. It's his whole life. How could you let all this noise—?'

Harry unfolded himself from the corner, where he was reading, and slipped indoors. Artemis put down her croquet mallet, stuck her chin in the air and announced that she was moving in with Ed completely. It had the effect Zoe would have predicted.

'You are punishing me,' said their mother tensely. 'This is because your father walked out on us.'

Artemis looked mutinous. Zoe flung herself out of the hammock and into the breach. As she always did.

'This is because Art's hormones are on full alert and Ed's cute,' she said patiently. 'Nothing personal.'

'Thanks, Zo,' said Ed, grinning.

Deborah Brown looked round distractedly. 'Where are my tablets?'

'Look, Ma,' said Artemis, stepping in between her and the pill packets in the house behind her, 'everyone lives with their boyfriend these days.'

Deborah seized the cue eagerly. 'Zoe doesn't.'

'Only because Zoe's got men coming out of her ears. She can't make up her mind,' said Artemis, quite convinced she was telling the truth.

Deborah didn't care. Ever since her husband had walked out she had had a pathological fear of change of any sort.

'I never interfere. You girls have your own flat up at the top of the house. Why can't things stay as they are?' Deborah's voice rose frantically.

'Because I want to grow up,' yelled Artemis, losing it.

So Zoe had to wade in and try to calm them both down. Artemis raged. Deborah gabbled maniacally, refusing to listen to anything either daughter said in case it sounded reasonable. It took the whole afternoon.

Then Artemis stamped out with a couple of cases and a sobered Ed beside her. Deborah took to her room and closed the curtains. And Zoe had time at last to finish her washing and get her clothes ready for the next day.

She was ironing a neat business shirt when Harry wandered in, back from wherever he had bolted to for sanctuary. She heard the front door and then he clattered down to the kitchen and stuck his head round the door.

'Bring out your dead. The place feels like a morgue. Where's Ma?'

'In her room.'

'Ah,' he said, understanding. 'A maternal moment?'

Zoe looked up and grinned. 'Horrible boy. Artemis has moved out. Ma's taken to her bed.'

Harry took the news with equanimity. 'Predictable.' He investigated the fridge. 'Is there anything to eat? I'm starving.'

'You can make yourself toast now, or I'll do scrambled eggs later.'

'I'm a growing boy. I can't live on scrambled eggs.'

Zoe sighed. 'Okay. Order in.' It was an extravagance, and money was tight. But her mother's housekeeping was erratic and Zoe's back-up food planning had gone awry this weekend.

Harry was gleeful. 'Great. Indian? Chinese? Italian?'

'Anything but pizza,' said Zoe, knowing that meant he would get crispy fried duck and plum sauce. 'And ask Ma if she wants some before you make the call.'

She finished ironing her shirt and hung it on a hanger before starting another one. Nothing of Harry's needed ironing, fortunately. As for Deborah, it was getting more and more difficult to get her to change her clothes at all. She would certainly not appreciate having her faded tee shirts pressed.

Zoe finished the ironing, folded the rest of the washing, threw away a pair of socks with holes in the toe and closed up the ironing board.

Harry came back from their mother's room, announced that Deborah was watching a video on her small television, and called in his order.

'One fried seaweed. One sesame prawn toast. Two egg fried rice. Crispy duck twice.'

Zoe bit back a smile.

He came off the phone and raised an eyebrow at the shirt on its hanger. 'Trying to impress?'

'Well, I was a bit rude to the new boss,' admitted Zoe. 'I'd like to—er—retrieve the position.' She twinkled. 'Actually, what I mean is I want to knock him cold. I've got a point to make.'

Harry sucked his teeth thoughtfully. 'Leave the top button undone,' he advised.

Zoe puffed. 'Thank you,' she said with irony.

'No, on second thoughts, make it two. These modern bosses take some impressing.'

'You'd know, of course, idle little toad.'

'I'm glad you brought that up. I've lined up a job for the summer.'

'Great,' said Zoe. 'What?'

But he only looked mysterious and refused to tell her. Zoe had effectively been substitute mother since Harry was ten. She knew enough not to push it.

Instead she got out plates and put them in the old-fashioned oven to warm.

'Harry—'

He was leafing through the television programmes. 'Yes?'

'Do you think everyone moves in with their boyfriend eventually?'

He looked alarmed. 'What has Naomi been saying?'

Naomi was his girlfriend.

'No, not you.' Zoe thought about it. 'Well, not yet anyway. I was thinking of, well, me.'

He laughed. 'The guy would have to work hard to get you to stick with him long enough to move in.'

'Yes,' agreed Zoe, depressed.

Harry thought about it. 'And Suze hasn't, has she? I mean Hermann's great, but she doesn't want to move to Germany, does she? She's still in that flat she wanted you to share?'

Zoe nodded, even more depressed. She had shared the flat with Suze for a few months after she came down from university. But first Artemis, then Harry had had their public exams, and Deborah had been locking herself away in her room and cooking family meals at midnight. There had been no choice, really.

'I don't think I'll be moving out again just yet,' she agreed brightly.

And added silently, *If ever.*

Monday morning was better. Zoe liked mornings anyway. Besides, she was always better when she had something to do.

And this morning what she had to do was show Jay Christopher that he had engaged a *treasure*. When she moved, as she would at the end of her contract, Jay Christopher was going to realise that he had made a big mistake by insulting her. A *big* mistake.

Zoe almost skipped into the cream and silver offices of Culp and Christopher. Jay Christopher, she thought, hugging herself, was in for the education of his life.

Though quite what she was going to do at Culp and Christopher nobody seemed to be sure. The Human Resources manager, a tall blonde, was manifestly not expecting her. She made a couple of investigative phone calls while trying to deliver a welcome spiel. It did not work very well.

'A degree in chemistry? Aren't you overqualified to temp?'

'Yes.'

What else did she expect her to say? thought Zoe, irritated. But the blonde was flustered by her brevity. She muttered a question into the telephone wedged under her ear and looked at the file in front of her.

'Er—yes. Well. So, do you think you're suited to the sort of work we do here?'

Zoe tried to be patient. 'That's why the Manoir Agency sent me.'

'Ah, but why did they choose you particularly?'

Zoe narrowed her eyes at her, losing patience. 'Just drew the short straw, I guess.'

Fortunately her answer fell on deaf ears. The telephone had obviously started broadcasting.

'Oh, it's Jay's doing, is it?' said the woman into the telephone. She made a note on her pad and then said, 'Right. I'll bring her along at ten.' She almost flung the phone down and turned back. 'Have you worked in public relations before, Zoe?'

'No,' Zoe admitted.

'Well, this is a very progressive company,' said the blonde, getting back on message with evident relief. 'We're committed to training. I'll make sure you go on one of the introductory talks that our chief gives. Jay Christopher,' she added unexpectedly, 'is just wicked.'

Zoe blinked. She thought of the man she had seen, tall as a tree and mad as a hornet. And up for a serious bit of re-education. She gulped. 'Wicked?'

Just what did that mean in a super-sophisticated office like Culp and Christopher? Zoe looked wildly out of the window and prayed for divine translation.

At home, with her twenty-year-old sister and seventeen-year-old brother, she knew what *wicked* meant. It was hip. It was far-out. It was wild. The ultimate compliment.

But that was in a house run for people who still spent their days in full-time classes and their nights dancing. The offices of Culp and Christopher Public Relations PLC were not like that. Culp and Christopher carried sophistication into a realm that made her eyeballs bubble.

The blonde, whose name she had been too nervous to catch, had already whisked her round so fast her toes had hardly touched the gleaming wooden floor. There were plenty of people milling about among the irregular geometric shapes that seemed to be desks. They were discussing their weekends, laughing, all friendly enough to the newcomer. But so far Zoe had understood less than half of the conversations she overheard. It was like travelling in foreign country. Who could guess what *wicked* meant in the realms of the super-cool?

The very grown-up super-cool, what was more. The blonde was wearing a dark grey trouser suit that was so well cut it seemed to flow into new shapes as she moved. It put Zoe's crisply ironed white shirt back where it belonged, on the bargain rack.

Oh, boy, am I out of my depth here.

And there was no way to disguise it. She gave up and asked, 'Wicked, like how?'

'You'll see,' said the blonde mysteriously.

That didn't help at all, of course.

'He's got a bad temper?' Zoe hazarded doubtfully.

She hoped that was what the blonde meant. Zoe knew about a lot about bad temper. She knew she could handle it, too. She wasn't sure how well she was going to handle the designer suits and the minimalist office.

The blonde grinned. 'Who knows?'

'What?'

'There was a movie we did some publicity for. *The Ice Volcano.* The girls started to call him that.'

Zoe blinked again. The man who wore flame silk shirts? *Ice?* This was worse than a foreign language. This was a foreign universe.

The blonde saw her confusion and laughed heartily. 'Jay is very, very self-contained. When he's angry he goes all cold and quiet. Brings the hair up on the back of your neck. Ice. Only then he explodes...'

She leaned back, smiling reminiscently. It was obviously a great show.

'Does he explode often?' said Zoe warily.

'Hardly ever. But when he goes, he goes. Once seen, never forgotten.'

'Oh.'

The blonde got to her feet. 'Probably won't happen while you're here. Don't worry about it. Come on. I'll show you where the hot negotiating goes on.'

She did, pointing out various framed photographs of products and personalities on the walls as they went. The photographs were all high quality, and some were truly beautiful. But they meant nothing to Zoe. There seemed to be a lot of sportsmen in fields or beautiful women standing in front of film posters.

The blonde was dry. 'Jay is very big in the sports world. It might be a good idea if you mug up before you meet him.'

I've already met him. He looked at me as if I were a slave he wasn't very interested in buying.

'I suppose so,' she said carefully.

'We'll tell Poppy. If he isn't in yet, she can give you his publicity file and you can learn it by heart.' She zipped Zoe down a narrow corridor, indicating doors briskly as they passed. 'Ladies' rest room. Supplies cupboard—everything that you want is in there: stationery, disks, printer cartridges, privacy, gossip. The kitchen. Boardroom.'

'I'll remember,' said Zoe, trying to commit the layout to memory. She thought there was a fifty-fifty chance that she would succeed.

The blonde pushed open another door. This one was studded with silver saucepan lids and led into a botanical hot house. Climbing plants and fig trees grew right up to the glass roof and the roof was *high*.

Instantly Zoe forgot the location of the stationery cupboard and the boardroom.

'Are there spiders in there?' she said involuntarily.

Her guide looked surprised. 'Never thought about it.'

'I bet there are. Hundreds of them. I *hate* spiders.'

'Don't worry, you won't be working in here. This is restricted territory. Jay's PA lives here. You don't get in without a visa.' She waved the note Suze had given Zoe to bring. 'Ah, here she is.'

For a moment Zoe wondered wildly if she were actually talking about a ten foot Swiss cheese plant. But then another tall blonde appeared from behind it. She was carrying a tiny trowel, with a gold handle, and had a pile of smart maroon laminated brochures stuffed precariously under her arm. She looked distracted.

'Hello, Isabel,' she said to Blonde Mark I, scattering brochures.

Ho. So they don't like each other. Zoe was good at interpreting tones of voice. She bent and gathered up the fallen brochures.

'Hi, Poppy,' said Blonde Mark I coldly. 'This is the girl from the agency I called you about. Zoe Brown. I've done the paperwork, but you'll know where Jay wants her to work.'

It was sweet enough. But so was poison, thought Zoe. Dislike was clearly mutual.

She sighed. She hated office wars. It was tough enough being a temp anyway, without having to work out departmental battle lines.

She said hastily, 'They said something about a research project? But I can file and do word processing as well.'

The blonde called Poppy looked taken aback. Isabel smiled maliciously.

'Your call,' she said. 'I don't know a thing about it. Suze at the temp agency said Jay rang through to her himself.'

'Then we'll ask Jay.'

Isabel went into exaggerated surprise. 'He in yet?'

'Er—no.'

Isabel grinned. 'Been to stay with the gardener bird, has he?'

Poppy narrowed perfectly made-up eyes at her adversary. *The Battle of the Blondes,* thought Zoe. She moved carefully out of range.

'I'm not discussing Jay's private life with you, Isabel Percy, so you can stop fishing. If you don't know what to do with her, you can leave Zoe here with me. I'm sure you've got plenty of work to do.'

Isabel recognised defeat. She shrugged and turned to Zoe.

'Sorry about that. If you need to talk, you know where I am. Human Resources, second floor.'

'Thank you,' said Zoe in a neutral voice. Rule One, when joining a new office, was be polite to everyone.

'Jay will tell you everything you need to know,' said Poppy quickly.

'It's still kind of you,' Zoe told Isabel. 'I appreciate it.' Rule Two was don't take sides.

Isabel raised a hand in farewell. 'Good luck. Don't get eaten by the spiders. See you around.'

She went.

The hard look went out of Poopy's face. She went back to faintly worried, which Zoe suspected was her habitual expression.

'Suze didn't say anything else about where you'd be working?' Poppy asked. 'Like research into what, for instance?'

Zoe shook her head. 'But I could start with Mr Christopher,' she said, mindful of Isabel Percy's advice. 'I obviously ought to know more about him and this agency than I do.'

'Of course.' Poppy looked relieved. She dived round a curtain of leaves so fat they looked as if they ate people. Had eaten several recently, in fact. Zoe followed, taking care not to brush against the plant in case it had teeth.

Behind it there was an oasis of relative normality.

'Wow,' said Zoe, forgetting Rule Three, never comment adversely on the working environment, 'a real desk. Drawers and a leg at each corner and everything.'

Poppy was rummaging through a pile of papers that leaned like the Tower of Pisa, but at that she looked up and grinned.

'Don't let the trendiness in the main office fool you. Culp and Christopher is as good as it gets. The trick desks are just for fun. Ah, here it is.'

She fished out a battered A4 folder. Zoe put the brochures she had harvested down on the desk and accepted it.

'Now, where are you going to sit? Probably not the boardroom; you never know who's going to use it. Um—what about Jay's waiting area?'

Zoe nodded obediently and settled into carved oak chair that looked at least four centuries out of step with the rest of the decor. She resisted the temptation to put her feet on a carved chest of similar design that served as a coffee table.

The folder proved to contain what looked like the draft material for a profile of Culp and Christopher Public Relations. Zoe looked at their client list with interest—she had worked for at least three of the large public companies who figured on it. But what was really intriguing was the staff—former newsmen, sports stars, politicians, even a token aristocrat.

Above all the stuff about Jay Christopher, Olympic medallist, adviser on track and field sports to a series of government bodies and all round public relations guru, made compelling reading. Hermann had said he was running with the great and the good, Zoe thought. Now she saw what he meant.

'Coffee?'

She looked up and found that Blonde Mark II was standing beside her, waving a glass jug. It steamed.

'Thank you,' said Zoe, surprised. Jay Christopher's PA ought to be too senior to get coffee for an incoming temp.

Her hostess fished a tall thin mug out from a disguised cupboard in the coffee table chest.

'Jay drinks the stuff by the tanker load. If you get desperate there's always coffee brewing in here.' She poured dark fragrant liquid into the futuristic crockery. 'He's passionate about it. If you give him half a chance he'll give you a history of coffee-drinking from the year dot.'

Privately Zoe doubted that the great man would give his new temp thirty seconds of his valuable time. Her father was a busy and ambitious man. On the whole it was a type she was not keen on.

'Milk? Sugar?'

Zoe shook her head.

Poppy did not disguise her relief. 'Good. Jay takes it black, no sugar. There are packets around here somewhere, but I can't always find them.' She poured some for herself and perched on the edge of the chest. 'Find anything interesting in there?'

'Well, now I know what a public relations company does, I think. And what a big cheese Jay Christopher is.'

'Well, that's an improvement,' said a cool dark voice from the doorway.

Zoe rocketed to her feet, spraying coffee widely. Poppy was unmoved. She got up more slowly and kept her cup horizontal.

'Hi, Jay. This is—'

'We've met,' he said crisply.

This morning he was wearing a soft dark suit even more beautifully cut than Isabel Percy's. The shirt underneath was imperial purple.

More silk, thought Zoe, eyeing it with mixed feelings. On the one hand she always wanted to touch silk, let it run through her fingers. On the other, she really, really did not want to touch Jay Christopher.

He was still tall, dark and handsome. Sexy as hell. And mad as a hornet?

He strode through the foliage to a door so discreet it was nearly invisible. 'Bring in the life-giving, Poppy, my love. And we'll see what Zoe has to offer Culp and Christopher. Other than her assessment of my place on the cheese index.'

Face rigid, Zoe followed.

He flung a small document case across the room so that it landed neatly on a glass coffee table and turned to her.

He was exactly as she had remembered, Zoe thought. In the light of day she could see that his skin was an even golden ochre and his eyes a strange greeny-hazel. But for the rest he was exactly what her nightmares had told her: too tall, too sleekly dark, too handsome. He even had a haughty nose and beautifully kept hands, which she had passed over on her last inventory of his assets. Well, face it, she had not got further than that controlled and passionate mouth.

She looked anywhere but at his mouth. 'If you remember, working here was not my idea,' she said with spirit.

She saw him put the irritation away from him like a jacket he'd taken off. He was no longer mad as a hornet. He was charming. Determinedly charming.

She watched the beguiling smile which put an indentation in one cheek and thought, *Your performance is nearly as good as mine.* The smile was—almost—irresistible. Zoe regarded him with total suspicion.

'Right. Now, what can you offer us?'

She outlined her office skills stiffly. All the more stiffly as he didn't seem to be listening very hard.

His smile grew. 'You really don't like me very much, do you?' he said.

Zoe breathed hard. 'Do I have to like you?'

He beamed. 'You'll do.'

Great. More and more like the slave market.

'Gee, thanks,' she said with heavy irony.

He ignored that. He slung himself down behind a light glass and chrome table and switched on a computer that he'd magicked out of a hidden wall cupboard. At once he was flicking away absently. He seemed to have no more than half an eye on the messages that flashed up on the screen and then disappeared.

'Not at all. Take a load off. Sit.'

It was not a gracious invitation but she was quite glad to comply. Her head was beginning to spin slightly.

'Thank you.'

He carried on scrolling through his messages on the screen. 'So. They showed you round? What do you think of the place?'

Zoe was taken aback. 'I don't know anything about public relations.'

'Neither do most of our customers. And they come through here all the time. I'm curious as to what they make of us. So, tell me, what were your first impressions?'

'Schizophrenia,' she said honestly.

He stopped flicking for a moment. 'What?' He sounded genuinely intrigued.

'Well, the decor—' She waved her hand. 'You don't seem to be able to make up your mind whether you want to be a set for a sci-fi film or the waiting room of Louis Quatorze.'

'Really?' He looked at her curiously. He did not seem offended. 'No one's ever said that before.'

'Maybe nobody has dared to.'

'You're a real original, aren't you?' He said it with the air of a connoisseur, as if she ought to be flattered by his approval.

She was not flattered. Suddenly, blessedly, she was hopping mad.

'Am I? Is that supposed to be compliment?'

Jay shrugged. 'I don't pay compliments. Especially not to women who work for me.'

'That must make for a happy work place,' said Zoe, bristling.

For a moment he looked startled. Then he smiled again, with a lot less conscious charm, she thought.

'Makes it peaceful, at least,' he said ruefully. 'Almost the only house rule we have. Don't screw the company. You can make private phone calls. I don't care what time you get in or leave, as long as you do your own work. But if you start a steaming affair with a colleague you get your cards and leave at the end of the week.'

Zoe was so angry she could have danced with temper if she had not been wearing her best clothes and trying to be dignified. 'What about an affair that's only slightly simmering?' she asked sweetly.

His eyes narrowed. 'A barrack room lawyer, are you? Fine. The definition is: any relationship that causes sheep's eyes across the computer.'

'And how do you define sheep's—?'

Suddenly he tired of the game. 'Anything other people notice,' he snapped.

'Oh, well, that's all right,' she said unwarily. 'I'm good at keeping things secret.'

When he was angry his eyes went a flat, brownish green, she thought. He looked at her for an unnerving, silent minute.

'Are you deliberately trying to provoke me into sacking you on your first day here?' he said at last softly.

She stood her ground. She had paid attention when Suze talked, after all.

'You can't afford to sack me. You won't get anyone else in the time and you've run out of good will in the agencies,' Zoe pointed out.

It was a stand-off. They glared at each other until the door opened and Poppy came in with a tray. She took in the atmosphere in one glance, put down the coffee, and backed out fast.

But it broke the tension.

'Come to think of it, how do you manage to get through staff so fast?' asked Zoe, bland as cream. 'Do they collapse on the treadmill?'

'They fall in love with me,' said Jay, even blander.

She gasped, gagged, and collapsed into a coughing fit.

His eyes lost that green angry look. He looked satisfied, damn him.

But he still had good manners. 'Would you like some water?'

She shook her head, eyes streaming. He passed her a neatly laundered handkerchief.

'That's the other house rule,' he said, pouring coffee while she mopped her eyes and got her breath back painfully. 'Never mind the end of the week. If you fall in love with me you leave at once. On the hour. Clear?'

He gave her the coffee cup. Zoe took it with a hand that was only just not trembling with rage.

I ironed my best shirt so this comedian could patronise me, she thought in fury.

She said aloud, 'No need to worry about that. I'm the original Hard-Hearted Hannah.'

He was pouring his own coffee, but at that he stopped and looked round. One eyebrow flicked up in amusement. 'No man gets to the fifth date with me,' she told him, smiling so hard her teeth hurt. 'Ask Suze. I don't fall in love.'

He pursed his lips in a silent whistle. It was disbelief incarnate. It was the last straw.

'I'm too easily bored.'

'Bored?' He did not sound pleased.

'Yes.' Zoe sipped her coffee. She was shaking with indignation but he would never have guessed it. Performing Zoe was in control again, and she was *good*. 'I agree with you. Office affairs are messy. And never worth it.'

His eyebrows flew up.

So he didn't like that, did he? Good! She could have hugged herself with glee.

She gave him her best hot babe smile, all eyes and intensity.

'So chill out, dude. You'd never be a candidate.'

CHAPTER FIVE

SO HE'D never be a candidate, wouldn't he? Ms Hip Chick was making a big mistake if she thought he'd ever *want* to be a candidate.

But even as the words formed in Jay's furious brain he was finding other words pushing them out of the way. And not just words.

Hell!

Wrong time. Wrong place. Wrong woman. Oh, boy, was she the wrong woman, with her curls that she couldn't keep under control and that spit-in-your-eye-as-soon-as-look-at-you manner.

He said it all to himself as he stared into her taunting brown eyes. Didn't make any difference. He still had to wrestle his libido back into its cave.

Down boy!

'Zoe Brown—' he began darkly.

She put a hand on her hip and tilted her head at him defiantly.

Hell and double hell.

Precision and self-control at all times, Jay reminded himself. That was what made success. Whether it was long-distance running or business, the same principle applied. You focused on one goal—*one*—and you tuned out all distractions. Zoe Brown was going to be harder to tune out than most, but he would do it. Oh, yes, he would do it.

If he could still run when he could no longer feel his legs and there was nothing but will driving him on, he could neutralise the impact of a voluptuous mouth and a bad attitude. Maybe he could even turn it to his advantage, now he came to think of it. After all, she really, *really* didn't like him. And most of her predecessors had liked him too much.

So he smiled blandly, straight into her hot eyes.

'That's a good start. Carry on hating me. That is definitely your unique selling point.'

'What?'

'It will compensate in full for your inexperience. Even for a certain amount of inefficiency.'

'I am not,' said Zoe between her teeth, 'inefficient.'

'No?' He was deliberately sceptical. Suze had told her to challenge the girl. She'd said that was the only way to knock the self-doubt out of her. Well, this was going to be the challenge of her life.

'If you'll just tell me what you want me to do, I'll even show you,' she told him, with a fierce smile.

He raised his eyebrows. 'Then come with me.'

She steamed beside him down to the open plan office so angry she could barely speak.

'Abby,' he said to a tall woman with soft dark hair and gentle eyes. 'Zoe is joining us. Point her in the direction of a computer, would you?'

'Sure, Jay.'

And to Zoe, 'I'm giving a keynote speech at a conference in Venice. Public Relations in a Changing World. I scribbled out some notes and left a list of things I wanted checked and updated. It's all on file.'

He seized a notepad off Abby's desk and scribbled down some words. He tore the page off and handed it to Zoe.

'There you are. That will get you into the file. Talk to me at the end of the day about how long it's going to take.'

He left.

Abby smiled at Zoe. 'I saw you earlier, didn't I? Welcome again.'

'Thank you.'

'That sounds like the stuff Banana was doing. Interesting. Well, look, take the desk under the window for now, and we'll get you logged on.'

The Venice file was enormous. More a rag-bag than a decent way of organising information, Zoe thought. She was pleased. This was what she was good at. She lost herself in archived magazine articles and forgot challenging Jay Christopher. Well, nearly.

She still knew who they meant when a voice above her head said, 'I hear the Volcano has gone up again.'

She looked up.

Abby was standing by her desk with a tall, fierce-looking woman in an eye-hurting magenta leather catsuit.

'Molly di Paretti,' said the woman, holding out a hand.

At least she wasn't another battling blonde, thought Zoe. She stood up and shook hands.

Molly di Paretti smiled and the ferocity disappeared. 'Abby and I are off to hit Patisserie Pauline. Coming?'

Well, Jay had said he didn't care what time she got in or left as long as she did her work. Presumably he did not care about expeditions in search of coffee, either.

'Great,' she said.

She saved her work and logged off without sitting down again. They went.

Patisserie Pauline turned out to be a small half-shop, with a bar along one wall and half a dozen marble-topped tables in its depths. It was full of the smell of coffee and warm pastry.

'Bliss,' said Molly.

'You're a carbohydrate junkie,' said Abby amused.

'Guilty.'

Zoe looked at the magenta catsuit and shook her head. 'With a figure like that?'

'I know,' said Abby. 'Life's not fair.'

'Look, I was heavy once. Then I lost it and learned to prioritise. One of Pauline's brioches is worth giving up fish and chips for.' Molly flicked an imperious finger at a round woman behind the counter. 'The usual, Pauline. Plus one for the new member.'

She led the way to the back of the shop, where people were already seated at all the tables but one. It had a little reserved notice in the middle. Molly flicked it off and put it on the counter behind her. She sat down. Zoe was not entirely sure that the table had been reserved for them, though. Molly had the look of a rule-breaker. Zoe was envious.

'Now,' said Molly, purple elbows on the table, leaning forward. 'Tell. What has he done with the body?'

Zoe recoiled, 'Body?'

Abby intervened. 'Molly's distorted sense of humour,' she explained. 'She means your predecessor. Banana Lessiter.'

Zoe began to feel as if she had broken through into another dimension. 'Banana?'

'Barbara Lessiter. She called herself Banana.' Molly was impatient. 'What's he done with her? She was still alive and lusting after him all over the office last Wednesday.'

'I *see*.' Zoe was suddenly enlightened. 'That must be why he warned me against falling in love with him.'

'He didn't!' The others stared at each other, between shock and amusement.

'Yes, he did. It's a dismissal matter, apparently. That must be what happened to—er—Banana.'

'You've got to be right,' agreed Molly. She whistled. 'Wow. She really must have got him running scared.'

Zoe choked. 'Scared? Jay Christopher? That's a joke, right?'

Molly shook her head. 'You have no idea. The man is—'

'A good boss and an all-round decent guy,' interrupted Abby reprovingly.

Molly was unrepentant. 'Oh, sure. But he never lets a woman get too close, either. Come on, Abby, admit it. He cares more about his art collection than he does about his girlfriends.'

'I don't know any of his girlfriends.'

'Well, you wouldn't, would you? He just told Zoe. It's the quickest way to get your cards.'

Zoe said slowly, 'He said there was a no dating policy for the whole office. Not just him. Is that true?'

Molly pulled a face.

But Abby said, 'Yes, there is. And I agree with it.'

'Emotions will be left in the umbrella stand,' muttered Molly.

Abby ignored her. 'It takes the pressure off. You can break up with your boyfriend and not have to make a choice between seeing him at the next desk every morning or leaving your job. Which,' she added tartly, 'if you went through men as fast as Molly used to, is a definite plus.'

Molly grinned.

Zoe winced inwardly. There were plenty of people ready to say that *she* went through men quite as fast as Molly could.

'Is that what Banana did?'

'Don't know what she did,' said Molly. 'Though, knowing her, it probably involved taking her clothes off. I mean we all let our hormones ride us sometimes, but Banana's galloped.'

Zoe winced again. And hid it, as she always did.

Here we go again. Another bunch of nice women who are going to rub my nose in it every time I turn round. Am I really the last virgin in captivity?

'Still, she wasn't subtle, but I gather she was effective. Until Jay, of course.'

'Poor Banana,' said gentle Abby.

Molly snorted. 'It's amazing he put up with her this long. She's been all over him since the Christmas party.'

Abby looked horrified suddenly. 'Oh, no! The party!'

'What?'

But their coffee arrived, along with a basket of mouthwatering pastries. By the time they had chosen, and tasted, and pronounced, Abby was easily able to change the subject. And she was desperate to do just that, Zoe saw. She wondered why. Molly and Abby seemed such friends!

Still, people were not necessarily all that they seemed. Self-effacing Abby turned out to be the woman the popular press called Fab Ab. She was married to an international tennis star turned businessman. Even Zoe, not a reader of the gossip columns, had heard of her. Maybe friendship was different in celebrity circles, thought Zoe, going quiet.

She did not have long to nurse her doubts. Abby cornered her in the luxurious ladies' restroom less than an hour later.

'Molly's getting married next month. Jay wants C&C to give her a surprise party. I just remembered it when we were having coffee. Trouble is—Banana was supposed to organise it.'

'Ah,' said Zoe, relieved that she had not misjudged Abby after all.

'If Jay's sacked her, I'll have to find out how far she's got and run with it.'

'Do you want me to have a trawl through her desk and see if she's left any notes?' Zoe offered. 'I've inherited her other files, after all.'

'Would you? That would be such a help. Molly's bound to get suspicious if she sees me rummaging through Banana's desk.'

'Sure thing. No problem.

Zoe took the desk drawers apart. There were notes. They showed that Banana had done precisely nothing except get a budget out of Jay Christopher and ring round a few restaurants. It was a generous budget, Zoe saw. You might not be allowed to fall in love with him, but he was lavish when he celebrated your falling in love with someone else. But there was still nowhere booked to hold the party.

'Help!' squeaked Abby, when she told her.

'Do you want me to do it?'

Abby was doubtful. 'You've only just got here.'

'I can handle it,' said Zoe with conviction. 'It will be a nice change from sorting and filing.'

'Then thank you,' said Abby with real gratitude. 'I'll give you the address list.'

Jay wandered through the open plan office around four. There was a comfortable buzz of activity. When he walked in, it neither revved up nor fell to ostentatious concentration. Jay noticed that with approval.

'Well?' he said, pausing by Tom Skellern's desk.

Tom was on the telephone to a City editor on behalf of a new client fighting off a takeover. He raised his thumb to Jay and continued with the conversation.

Jay turned to the next desk. 'Molly?'

'If you're asking about Zoe Brown, she'll be okay,' said Molly crisply. 'Abby will look after her. She's a nurturer.'

He pursed his lips. 'You think Zoe Brown needs looking after? I'd have said that she was more than capable of taking care of herself.'

'Now we've found her a computer and somewhere to sit, she probably is,' Molly said dryly. 'It would have helped if we'd known she was coming.'

'But we're supposed to be good at handling the unexpected, Molly. That's what public relations is all about,' he told her blandly.

'Ho, yus?' said Molly, roused. 'Well, you really got the gold medal for the way you handled Banana, didn't you?'

Zoe had just come back into the office. Jay caught sight of her. There was no doubt about it. The woman would be trouble on wheels if he gave her half a chance. But she moved like a dancer. He liked that. Pure aesthetic appreciation, he assured himself.

'What?' he said absently.

'Banana Lessiter? Remember? She used to work here until she clearly did something unexpected. We were asking ourselves where you had buried the body. Weren't we, Zoe?'

Arriving, Zoe stopped dead, startled. Jay gave her a wide, charming smile.

'Barbara has moved on to follow a new interesting career opportunity,' he said fluently. He was still smiling at Zoe. 'How does your first day feel?'

'Fine,' she said warily. She did not trust men who smiled straight into your eyes. Especially when that smile could charm birds off the trees and they knew it. And when they had told you that hating them was your unique selling point. Did Jay want to test exactly how immune she was to him? 'So far I'm doing just fine.'

Oh, yes, she would certainly do fine, thought Jay. He was giving her the full wattage and all she did was stand beside her desk and narrow her eyes at him. At a comparable stage in her employment Barbara Lessiter had started leaving crucial buttons on her shirt undone. And Barbara Lessiter was not alone. Zoe Brown was definitely a find.

So why did he feel annoyed? Even outraged? He did not want her to melt when he looked at her, after all.

He pulled himself together. 'Have you looked at the file? Do you know what you're doing yet?'

Abby had guided Zoe through more than the ladies' rest room and her predecessor's files. In the last two hours Zoe had read every speech Jay had made to the industry this last year. He seemed to make a lot of speeches.

'"Advertising stimulates the appetite. Public relations focuses a spotlight",' Zoe chanted.

Jay raised his eyebrows. 'Quoting me already?'

'Seems like a good idea,' said Zoe with composure.

He grinned. 'They've been telling you I'm a despot.'

Molly raised her eyes to the ceiling eloquently.

'Don't worry, Moll. I can take it,' he told her comfortably. And, to Zoe, 'I prefer to think of myself as an oligarch. An enlightened oligarch, of course. What I say goes. But what I say is reasonable.' He looked round at the others. 'Right?'

There was a chorus of ironic agreement. Jay's grin widened.

'And to prove how enlightened I am, you can ask Banana Lessiter to the next office party,' he said generously. 'And I won't say a word.'

But he said several words when Tom Skellern cornered him in his office a week later.

'I'm in love,' he announced exuberantly.

Jay grinned. Tom was an old fashioned chivalrous knight under his dark glasses and designer suiting. 'Congratulations.'

'With Zoe Brown. The new girl.'

Jay stopped grinning. He did not like that at all.

He said warningly. 'Tom, you know the rule. Just because you're up for a directorship—'

'That's why I'm in love,' said Tom impatiently. 'I've been doing the Hyder-Schelling tests on her. And she's perfect.'

'Why on earth have you been doing recruitment tests on Zoe Brown? We've already recruited her.'

'Yes, but just to do your dogsbodying for Venice.' Tom sat on the corner of his desk, suddenly serious. 'If we're going into this merger, we've got to boost our in-house research and response capacity. Otherwise Karlsson will swamp us. I've been roughing out a profile—and Zoe Brown fits it to a tee.'

Jay's eyes narrowed. 'Does she know you've been doing psychological tests on her?'

Tom was hurt. 'Of course. And not just her. All the girls. They thought it was fun.'

Jay was still not happy. He sighed, and said with palpable reluctance, 'Okay. Show me what you've got.' He held out his hand for the sheets.

Tom stabbed a finger at the top one.

'Look. Look at that score. She's total woman. She nurtures. She plans. She budgets. She takes her time to react. She thinks logic is not wholly reliable. She daydreams. She reads romance. Hell, she even knows how to cook—look…"to make a bread and butter pudding, butter slices of bread on both sides, whisk two whole eggs and a yolk in a pint of full cream milk—"'

'Give it here,' said Jay, whipping it out of his hand. 'You've been doing it again, haven't you? Slipping the Tom Skellern Ideal Wife Test in with the multiple choice questions.'

Tom laughed. 'It's important that they show initiative. Any monkey can tick multiple choice.'

'Tom—'

'Look, we agreed that we needed a really female female, didn't we? Especially if we're going to take this merger thing seriously. All those kooks in Karlsson are high on ambition and the need to prove they can drink more beer than we can. That's not the market.'

'It's a big segment of the market.'

'But not *all*. Don't the nurturers and the dreamers get a vote any more?'

'And you think Zoe Brown is a nurturer and a dreamer?' Jay said slowly.

'I know she is. The Hyder-Schelling tests cannot lie. Besides,' he added wickedly, 'she brightens the place up. Have you seen the red boob tube yet?'

Jay threw the sheets down. 'I'm not employing a woman because you want to go to bed with her bread and butter pudding. And that's final.'

Zoe saw a lot of Jay. Every time he came back into the office, from Brussels, or Manchester, or even a trip just down the road to Westminster, he summoned her into his office.

'Poppy and Isabel will put you top of their hit list,' teased Molly. 'The Battle of the Blondes escalates.'

For once Zoe did not laugh, though normally she enjoyed Molly's cynicism as much as anyone. And she was responsible for dubbing the inter-office rivalry the Battle of the Blondes, after all.

'It's nothing personal. It's just because I'm working on this speech, of course,' she told them seriously at Patisserie Pauline. 'It's only ten days away now. He's in a flap about it.'

'A flap? Jay?' Molly shook her head. 'I don't think so.'

But Abby shook her head. 'He's probably feeling guilty. It's a big honour to be asked. He should have done it months ago. Banana really let him down there.'

Zoe was intrigued by the woman about whom she had heard so much.

'What was she like?' she asked.

Abby shrugged. 'Used to be Molly's assistant. Did the music business, mainly. Wasn't here long. I didn't know her well.' She thought about it. 'Very hip. Very temperamental.'

'What do you think, Moll?'

'I think she should have kept her hormones in her handbag,' said Molly crisply.

Yet the girl who turned up at the private room in the Pacific Grill Rooms for Molly's surprise party didn't look temperamental. She didn't look like a case of galloping hormones, either. She wore designer rags that left some surprising bits naked to the air, and she was as tottery as a young antelope on her massive heels.

Zoe could not help herself. 'That's the man-eater?' she said, astonished.

'That's the one,' said Abby. 'Wouldn't think it to look at her, would you?'

The antelope had eyelashes that would have made Bambi sick with envy. She cornered Jay and used them to great effect.

'Oh, I don't know,' said Zoe.

Jay got the antelope a drink, made his excuses and walked away. Banana was the only woman in the world Zoe had ever seen pout prettily. Mind you, that could have been the wide innocent blue eyes that went with it.

Innocent. Huh! I bet she knows more than I do about just about everything.

The antelope stopped pouting and looked round for company.

'Hi,' she said, descending on Abby and Zoe. 'What a horrible boss you have.' She sounded envious. 'Still, at least he forgave me enough to let me come.'

She was also the only woman Zoe had ever known to drink a margarita and chatter breathlessly at the same time. How did she do that?

'What did you do to him, Banana?' asked Abby. She was no gossip, but she was as intrigued as everyone else.

The antelope was not offended. She shrugged. 'Waited till everyone had gone home. Went into his office with a bottle of champagne and some cushions.'

She finished her cocktail and replaced the empty glass with a full one from a passing waiter.

She did not stop talking. She did not even look at the tray. Just identified the slim glass stem by touch alone.

Experience, thought Zoe in unwilling admiration. *Drinks, men—she can handle the lot.*

'Hey, you only live once,' Banana went on. 'That's what I told him.'

Abby shook her head, mock astonished. 'How did he manage to hold out?'

'You tell me,' said Banana, unaware of mockery. 'I think he must be afraid of his emotions. Or women.'

Abby choked. Even Zoe, who had only a few weeks' acquaintance with Jay Christopher to judge by, boggled a bit.

Banana noticed that she was being teased at last. 'Well?' she challenged them. *'Well?'*

Abby flung up her hands. 'Pass. I'd have said that Jay was pretty enthusiastic about women. But maybe he's over-compensating.'

'Now you're being ridiculous,' Banana said loftily.

The party was getting noisy. The band was setting up. Banana reached for her third margarita, gave them both a vague smile, and limboed off in the direction of Tom Skellern.

Abby looked after her with amazement. 'What is she like? Cushions and champagne! I'm surprised Jay didn't have a seizure laughing at her.'

'Er—yes.'

'You wouldn't think she was a kid on her first date. Someone should tell her that grown-up men like to do their own hunting.'

Zoe tensed. *Here we go again,* she thought. *Performance Zoe, you're on stage again.*

'And not get their prey too soon,' she said lightly.

They exchanged world-weary looks and Abby laughed. Another one successfully convinced, thought Zoe, wondering why she bothered.

Yet it was so easy. That was the interesting thing about really sophisticated people. They had their own rules. If you were used to living a lie anyway, you picked up what new people expected *fast*. There was not a single person at the Culp and Christopher party who would have noticed that there was any difference between Zoe Brown and themselves.

Except Zoe Brown.

She danced and circulated and laughed at the in-jokes tirelessly. She was pleased with her performance.

Jay even congratulated her. 'You,' he told her, doing that full spotlight smile thing again, 'are one of my better discoveries. Come and dance with me, Discovery.'

He took her onto the floor for an energetic bop. He did not touch her—much. But he made her feel as if she was dancing with an expert. And that she was an expert, too.

When the music modified into a slow dance he returned her to a stool at the bar and summoned the overworked barman. By sheer force of personality, as far as Zoe could tell.

'That's a good trick,' she said dryly.

His eyes glinted. 'Isn't it? He knows a good customer when he sees one. What are you drinking?'

'Fizzy water,' said Zoe firmly.

She was intending to stay with Suze in her Kensington pad tonight. That meant going home on the night bus. She had stopped swigging alcohol an hour ago. The bus was fine, but you needed your wits about you, given the way it swayed as it whipped through the traffic-free streets. She had slept through the stop outside Suze's elegant street several times before she'd learned that. These days she paced her party drinking carefully.

He did not try and talk her out of it. He gave the order, asking for a glass of red wine for himself, she saw.

'Abby tells me you put this party together on your own,' he told her. 'Good work.'

Zoe accepted the compliment without excitement. 'I have a younger brother and sister. I can do parties.'

And how true that was! Well, other people's parties anyway.

He did not pick up that there was anything wrong. He said enthusiastically, 'You certainly can. And Molly didn't suspect a thing.'

On the dance floor Molly di Paretti was slow-dancing dreamily with the man she was going to marry. She looked as if she belonged in his arms, and they both knew it.

'She looks happy, doesn't she?' Zoe hadn't meant to sound wistful. Hadn't known she even felt wistful until she heard some note in her voice that shouldn't have been there. Not if she was having this great time that she was telling herself she was.

Jay must have heard it, too. He cocked his head.

'Don't go broody on me, Discovery,' he said in mock alarm.

Zoe pulled herself together. 'Broody? Me? Nonsense. I'm a party girl.'

He laughed, clearly convinced. And delighted about it.

His next words told her why. 'Yes, Suze told me your men don't last long. Never felt the urge to pair-bond?'

Zoe did not allow herself to wince. She said carefully, 'I just like to keep my options open.'

'You're a girl after my own heart.'

'So I hear,' she said acidly.

He might have turned down Barbara Lessiter. He might outlaw inter-office relationships. But everyone knew that he was a serial flirt. Even if the battling blondes hadn't been willing to pour out all the gossip Zoe would have worked it out from his press cuttings.

Every time he gave a speech he got his photograph in the paper. In every photograph, as far as she could see, he was escorting a different woman. All beautiful, all elegant. And all different.

According to Isabel of Human Resources, he had just dumped the latest girlfriend, too. Apparently she was a television gardening expert who was unusually gorgeous and had been getting stacks of fan mail ever since she'd walked into a hosepipe spray by mistake.

Poppy, bristling with secretarial discretion, had said that she did not know anything about that, implying the reverse.

Isabel had ignored her. 'She asked him for a commitment and he walked. She's absolutely broken-hearted,' she'd told the ladies' rest room.

Poppy had sniffed. 'Probably just had her head turned by the publicity. They never lived together, you know.'

Then she'd looked annoyed with herself for having betrayed so much.

'No, he never lets a woman get that close,' Isabel had agreed, restraining her triumph, but only just. 'Doesn't even stay the whole night, they say.'

Silence had fallen. They'd all shivered. The sheer aridity of it had chilled them all. Poppy and Isabel had exchanged half-ashamed glances, their rivalry momentarily overtaken.

Every woman there was thinking the same thing, thought Zoe. Every single one of them was thinking, There but for the grace of God go I.

So now she looked at Jay with unflattering steadiness.

'Hey,' he said mock alarmed. 'I'm no Bluebeard. I just don't make promises I can't keep.'

Zoe recognised that. She nodded. 'Nor do I,' she said fairly.

'There you are, then. We're the same, you and I.'

She bit back self-mocking laughter. *If only he knew!* 'I doubt it.'

'Oh, but we are. And the world envies us. It's the twenty-first century metropolitan dream.'

'Life as one long party?' she said sceptically.

He said coolly, 'Recreational sex and no responsibilities. That's what everyone wants really. The pair-bonders—' he nodded at Molly, now rubbing her cheek against her George's shoulder '—are the oddballs.'

Zoe looked across at them almost angrily. 'Is it being an oddball to be honest about your feelings?'

Jay studied her curiously. 'I don't tell lies about feelings. I—'

She snapped her attention back to him. She was shaking with an odd sort of grieving anger. 'Set the rules?' she supplied sweetly. 'No sex in the office. No commitments outside it. You're the sort of man who thinks that if he doesn't stay the night he's made the terms of the contract clear.'

His eyebrows twitched together.

'You've been listening to gossip,' he said, perfectly pleasantly. But suddenly he wasn't laughing any more.

Zoe could have kicked herself. But she was not a liar. Well, not about that sort of thing. And she was not a coward, either. She lifted her chin.

'Is gossip wrong, then?'

There was a pause. The party noises screeched on all around them. But Zoe had the distinct impression Jay was not hearing them. His high cheek-boned face looked suddenly pinched, as if he were cold. Or in pain.

'No,' he said at last, curtly.

She spread her hands. *Case proved*, they said, as clearly as words.

That was when Banana Lessiter staggered out of the gyrating crowd and made an unsteady beeline for Jay.

'Oh, Lord,' said Jay under his breath.

'I don't know what you're worried about,' Zoe said maliciously. 'I don't think she's into pair-bonding in a big way. She doesn't even work for you any more.'

'That's what worries me,' said Jay. He looked harassed. But the acid-bitten look had gone. 'Sorry, but you're on your own in this one. I've fought her off twice so far this evening. This is where the true gentleman takes evasive action.'

Smooth as an eel, he slid among the dancers. By the time Banana got to the bar he was not even visible in the crowd.

'Where's he gone?' she demanded, slurring a little.

'Evasive manoeuvres,' said Zoe truthfully.

'But I wan' him to dance with me.'

'I think he sort of guessed that.'

The girl looked at her, uncomprehending. 'Dance,' she said, and smacked her fist on the bar. 'Dance. Dance. Dance.' With every thump of her fist she swayed a little bit further from the vertical.

'I rather doubt it,' said Zoe. 'Why don't you sit down and have a coffee?' She waved at the barman, who was deep in conversation and not looking. 'And a glass of water. Several glasses.'

Banana seemed to think well of the idea. She began to hoist herself onto one of the tall bar stools. And then just seemed to give up midway. For half a second it looked as if she might make it, getting half a buttock onto the seat. But then gravity and two spaghetti legs took over. She put her hand to head and folded up as neatly as a concertina.

Zoe was off her bar stool before she knew it. She pulled Banana clear of the fallen bar stool and turned her on her side. She had another go at attracting the attention of the barman. But, crouching on the floor, she had even less success.

To her surprise, Jay arrived, speeding out of the crowd as if he was on rollerskates.

'What's wrong? Has she taken something?' He felt her forehead. 'Clammy.'

Zoe had seen this before. She had seen Harry through more than one encounter with serious alcohol while her mother watched old videos in her room.

'Too much to drink, I guess. She was swigging back margaritas earlier.'

'Damn. She told me it was the first time she had had them. I should have realised and stopped her.'

Across the prone body, Zoe raised her eyebrows. 'Do you think you could have? Banana seemed pretty determined to get her own way to me.'

He had that cold look back. 'Yes, I could.' He sounded angry. More with himself than anyone else, she thought. 'Too late to think about that now, though. What she needs is water. Then hospital, I suppose. Just in case she really has drunk enough to make this alcohol poisoning.' He had more success with the barman. 'Hey, Derek. Chuck us over a jug of water.'

The barman did.

Jay propped the girl up while Zoe dribbled water between her lips. Remembering Harry, flopping and incapable at fifteen, she massaged the girl's throat to make her swallow. Eventually her eyelids began to flutter and she moaned.

The barman was hanging over them by then, along with several of the other guests.

Jay took charge. 'Nothing to worry about, guys. Party on. I'll see she gets home safe.' And then, when they had gone back to the dancing, he said quietly, 'Call us a cab, will you, Derek? Zoe, can you help me with her?'

'Sure.'

It was gone three when they got her into the Accident and Emergency Department of a big London teaching hospital. The waiting room was almost empty. A weary-eyed triage nurse assessed Banana's state and whipped her straight into a cubicle. Unpleasant noises ensued.

Jay grimaced. 'Looks like we got here just in time.'

'At least if she's sick they won't have to pump her stomach,' said Zoe practically.

That surprised a choke of laughter out of him. 'Tell me, do you always look on the bright side?'

'No point in doing anything else.'

The receptionist at the glass-walled desk beckoned them over. 'Just a few details…'

Between them they did not know much. But then Zoe had the idea of looking through the girl's sequined evening purse. It contained her small pocket diary and gave her home address and assorted details, including her blood group and the fact that she had no allergies.

'Pity she didn't remind herself that alcohol was poison at the same time,' said Zoe acidly.

'Oh, I don't know.' He was maddeningly tolerant. 'She's just young and inexperienced.'

'Huh!' That caught her on the raw. She said unwarily, 'Still, I suppose it's better than being old and inexperienced.'

'This will teach her a valuable lesson—'

Another nurse was coming towards them.

'Can you tell me something about her? And this party tonight? When did she last eat? Is she likely to have taken recreational drugs?'

Jay shook his head. 'Not at any party of mine.'

'But maybe someone brought something that you didn't know about—'

'These guys work for me. They wouldn't risk it.'

Looking at the set of his mouth, Zoe found she believed him.

So did the nurse, evidently. 'Well, it could just be too much to drink. I'll tell the doctor.' She disappeared.

Zoe suddenly began to feel immensely tired. As if he sensed it, Jay put an arm around her and steered her towards a bench against a wall. He pushed her gently onto it and stood back, looking down at her with concern.

'Like a coffee?'

She smiled palely. 'Out of a machine? No, thank you.'

'Snob,' he said peacefully. 'Does it matter if it's wet and warm?'

'I'm not cold.'

And she was not. The harsh hospital lighting made everything seem dreamlike. She was neither hot nor cold, nor awake nor asleep, but floating somewhere in the suspended animation of near exhaustion.

'You're wiped, aren't you?'

She closed her eyes. 'I've been up since five. How long before that means I've been awake for twenty-four hours?'

He was startled. '*Five?* Why on earth—?'

'My brother has finished his exams. He's got himself a summer job. Guiding field trips for schoolchildren. He'd never have got himself out of the house if I hadn't. Afterwards I couldn't go back to sleep. So I did some housework.'

'And then you ran around preparing my Venice paper all day. And ran the party all night. Topping it off with a crisis.' He sounded remorseful. 'Poor old Discovery. You really are a tower of strength, aren't you?'

Zoe pulled a face. 'You really know how to flatter a girl.'

He shook his head. 'No flattery. I told you. I tell the truth.'

And quite suddenly it was all too much for her. All the deceit and the games and the feeling of everything getting away from her. She just didn't want it any more. She was so *tired* of it.

She said baldly, 'Well, I don't.'

He went very still.

'I've not been telling the truth so long that when I try I can't do it.'

Zoe tipped her head back against the wall. The harsh light made her eyelids ache. She stared at the ceiling almost dreamily. She felt as if she were in free fall, as if all the conventions and pleasant, safe habits of every day had fallen away. All the rules, too.

She said in a flat voice, 'Don't run away with the idea that you know one single thing about me. You don't.'

Jay sat down on the bench beside her, carefully not touching her. But she could feel him watching.

'Want to tell me about it?' he said quietly.

And quite suddenly she did. Well, she wanted to tell *someone*.

There was no reason in the world why she should tell Jay, of course. She didn't know him. What she did know she didn't like. He was serial flirt with a tough break-up technique and no conscience. Or that was what they said. It seemed to be true. He was the last person in the world she would have expected to confide in.

But the small hours, the nearly empty waiting area, and those fierce lights seemed to have got her spaced out quite as much as any recreational drug would have done.

He was also her boss and the owner of Culp and Christopher. Which meant he paid her salary. You didn't tell things you wouldn't tell—hadn't told—your best friend to a man like that, did you?

Of course you didn't. It was crazy.

Knowing it was crazy, Zoe watched a fly walk across the ceiling towards one of the panels of white light and said idly, 'You remember those oddballs we were talking about earlier?'

'Lovebirds and pair-bonders?' he said in a still voice. 'Are you telling me you're secretly married, Discovery?'

A little laugh shook her.

'No. Odder than that. Sorry, Jay, you've got a *real* weirdo on your hands this time. I'm a virgin.'

CHAPTER SIX

JAY stared at her. She did not look at him. Her eyes were fixed dreamily on the ceiling. She looked tired to death. But she did not look as if she was drunk. Or lying.

He said cautiously, 'Is this a wind-up?' Of course she could have gone mad. 'You're telling me you're—er—untouched by human hand?'

Zoe's tired eyes lit with a rueful smile. 'Yup. That's about the size of it.'

Jay saw the smile with relief. Well, at least she wasn't completely barking yet. He thought about what she had said for several moments.

At last he said, 'Why?'

She avoided his eyes. It did not take much to work out that she was embarrassed. Covering it well, but embarrassed all the same.

Another argument for her sanity, judged Jay. He thought fast. Undoubted sanity made her claim all the more odd.

She was gorgeous. She was funny. She was sensible. She *could* not be a virgin. Not in metropolitan London in the twenty-first century.

She saw his disbelief. Her eyes slid away from his. 'I suppose I just—never got round to it.'

'Ah.' Curiouser and curiouser. 'But actually I meant—why tell *me*?'

She flushed faintly. 'Oh. Sorry. That.' She considered. 'You said, *Want to tell me about it?* People don't usually say that to me,' she said simply.

Jay stared. 'What?'

'I don't have crises. My friends and family have lots. So I'm the one who listens.'

He nodded slowly. 'Makes sense.'

It didn't. It had to be a lot more complicated than that. But now was not the time to point it out. Not if he wanted her to carry on confiding.

Jay was astonished at how much he wanted her to confide in him.

She gave a rueful laugh. 'You're kind, aren't you?' She sounded surprised.

'Is that so unbelievable?' said Jay, wounded. Then, hurriedly, as she opened her mouth, 'Don't answer that.'

She smiled, more easily this time. 'Well, you have to admit, you did warn me against—er—intimacy. You said it was a sacking offence.'

'I didn't mean you weren't allowed to tell me things.'

'Didn't you?' Her eyes were shadowed. 'But that's the start of intimacy, isn't it? Telling someone something private. Something—special. Something you don't want to tell the world.'

Was that she what she had done? Told him something she didn't want to tell the world?

Yes, he thought. Suddenly he felt ten feet tall.

Aloud, he said, 'When I warned you off, I'm afraid I was thinking of something a bit more basic. It included sending me overheated e-mails and trying to get my clothes off.'

'Oh!'

He smiled at her, straight into her eyes, the way he always did to women who moved him. 'As long as you keep your hands to yourself, you can tell me anything you want to.'

But she wasn't noticing the penetrating smile. She was too busy picking over her own part in the conversation.

She shook her head ruefully. 'It doesn't begin to make sense. Why on earth would I start unloading on a man who pays my salary? It's not only unprofessional, it's a quick and easy way to talk myself out of a job.'

He realised, suddenly, that he had not been thinking of her as an employee for hours. Even before she had dropped her confiding bombshell. Certainly he would never have said, *Want to tell me about it?* to Barbara Lessiter. Or anyone else in the office, probably.

It started another idea running. Not a welcome one.

'Do you *want* to talk yourself out of a job?'

'Oh.' Zoe looked astonished. 'No, of course not. I like what I do. I like helping Abby and Molly and Tom. I like doing your research. I was even wondering if there might be a chance of a permanent job—' She broke off, flushing deeper. 'No, I didn't mean that. Hell, I'm being stupid tonight.'

She jumped up and walked about the overlit room for a bit.

She was making a valiant attempt to curb it but she looked really upset. He saw that she was biting her lip and she was frowning.

Jay did not say anything. But he was relieved that she did not want to leave him. Hugely relieved. He was not quite sure why. It seemed out of all proportion.

Though Zoe Brown was good at her job, no question. One of the best they'd ever had, in fact. But even so—when had he last cared enough about whether someone joined the firm to hold his breath in case they turned him down?

He did not like the implications of that. He put it out of his mind. Now was the time to address himself to immediate problems, he thought. That was what he was good at: problem-solving. He brought his cellphone out of his pocket and went into practical mode.

Eventually Zoe stopped pacing and came and stood in front of him. She looked oddly young and brave, in her tired party gear.

'I'm sorry. This is the last time and place to start hustling for a job. I apologise,' she said formally.

He was not going to let her see his relief. Of course he wasn't. Especially as he was not sure where it came from. He didn't share things he didn't understand.

Instead he gave her one of his best knock-'em-dead smiles. Not the one for women who moved him. The one for women he wanted—needed—to charm.

'I agree. We'll talk about the job in the office.'

He meant, *And now we'll talk about you and your extraordinary announcement*. Only she took it as a rebuke. She hardly seemed to notice the high-voltage charm. Instead, she looked away.

'Okay,' she said in a constrained voice.

Then the nurse came back with the doctor. And it was too late to explain that he hated the idea of her leaving.

They were intending to keep Ms Lessiter in for observation for twenty-four hours, they said. They thought it was just the drink, but they weren't quite sure what was going on. And as they could find her a bed—for once—they would run some more tests in the morning.

Jay nodded. 'And after that? Will she need to be looked after?'

The doctor grinned. 'My guess is that she'll have the mother and father of a hangover and the ward staff will give her hell. Apart from that she should be fine. This is just a precaution.'

Jay nodded. 'Keep me posted.' He fished out one of his business cards. 'If there's anything wrong I will get in touch with her family. But they don't live in London. And I don't see much point in letting them know their daughter has been partying too hard, do you? Not if that's all it is.'

The nurse took the business card.

'So you're not—er—her partner?'

'Former employer,' said Jay briefly. 'And—before you ask—I'm not doing cold compresses and warm drinks for Banana Lessiter. It wouldn't be safe. If she needs nursing I'll pay for it. But that's where my responsibility stops.'

The nurse looked rather shocked, but the doctor laughed. 'It shouldn't come to that. But call tomorrow and she can tell you herself.'

Jay hesitated. 'Can we see her?'

'If you like. She's making sense of a sort.'

She was making enough sense to rear up from her hospital trolley and fling herself onto Jay's breast.

'Take me home. I wanna take your clothes off...'

Zoe blenched, and even the tolerant doctor looked taken aback. Only Jay was unmoved. He detached the girl's indecently busy hands without fuss.

'We've been through this before,' he said calmly. 'Thanks, but no thanks.'

'But I wanna—'

'Got it,' said Jay. 'You want. I don't. No room for negotiation on this one. Sorry and all that.'

The doctor looked at him with admiration bordering on awe. 'She does this often?'

Jay stepped back and checked the fastenings of his clothes. 'Couple of times. She hasn't been tanked out of her head before,' he added fair-mindedly. 'But she wasn't listening to reason, either. The only thing is to say no and keep on saying it as you back out of the door.'

They exchanged a look of total masculine comprehension.

'I'll bear it in mind,' said the doctor. He sounded as if he meant it.

Banana let out a wail like a thwarted six-year-old. The nurse urged her down again, repressing a smile.

'Relax. A porter will be taking you up to the ward in a few minutes.'

Jay looked at Zoe. 'Well, that seems to let us off the hook. Coming?'

She said goodbye to Banana, who ignored her, and followed him out of the hospital.

'I'll have to find the bus stop for—'

'I'll take you home, of course,' he said, shocked.

'And how are you going to do that?' she said dryly.

He stepped out of the brightly lit entrance. In the darkness an engine switched on. From the shadows a car detached itself and slid up to the kerb in front of them. Zoe stared at it, half-astonished, half-annoyed.

'Don't tell me. You're a magician.'

Jay shook his head. 'Just a guy with a cell-phone and a friendly limo service,' he told her solemnly.

'A friendly limo service that follows you around after dark?'

He laughed aloud at that. 'No. They already knew I'd need a car some time tonight. I just called them when you were pacing around back there.'

'Oh.'

He opened the door behind the chauffeur for her. 'Where am I taking you?'

She gave him the address.

It was not what he was expecting. Annoyed with this further failure on the part of his office administration, he raised his eyebrows. 'I thought you lived in North London?'

He saw that she was surprised. 'I do. But when I know I'm going to be out really late I beg a bed for the night from a friend. No taxi driver in the known world wants to go to Muswell Hill after midnight.'

'Ah.'

He closed the door behind her and gave the address to the driver. Then went round the car and got in beside her. It was a big car. He had room to stretch out his long legs. There was also plenty of room on the back seat. And if Zoe did not exactly huddle in the corner—well, she made sure that there were several cubic feet of air space between their bodies.

Jay did not like that.

'Relax,' he said acidly. 'I'm not going to sack you just because our shoulders happen to touch.'

She tensed. He could feel it. But not because she was cowed.

'That's a relief,' she retorted. 'Is it all right if I have it in writing?'

Jay smiled to himself in the dark. That was his Zoe, coming out fighting.

'On your desk Monday morning,' he assured her.

He stretched comfortably, letting his arm extend along the back of her seat. She sent him a sideways look. He caught the turn of her head. 'I'm counting on it,' she said coolly.

And she turned in the seat so that she was almost facing him and his fingers did not reach her shoulder.

Oh, yes, she was fighting her corner, all right. Jay watched her as they flashed through intermittent light from the darkened streets.

'So who's the friend?' he said lazily.

He felt her jump. He saw the bright glint of eyes before her lashes veiled them.

'Oh—Suze.'

'Ah, Susan. Of course.' It was stupid to be relieved that the friend's flat she went back to did not belong to man. It had nothing to do with him who she dated, after all. But he was relieved. He couldn't deny it.

'She's my oldest friend. She brought you to our party,' she reminded him.

'I remember. She must be quite a bit older than you.'

Zoe sighed. 'I'm twenty-three. Suze is twenty-four.'

'Ah, but Susan was born forty. A sophisticated forty.' He added thoughtfully, 'Which makes her about five years younger than my friend

Hermann. Otherwise I'd be worried by the age difference.'

Zoe chuckled involuntarily. 'I know what you mean.'

He looked at her curiously. He wished he could make out her expression. 'I wouldn't have thought you had much in common.'

'You'd be wrong. We went to school together. We've seen each other through a lot.'

'Ah.'

He badly wanted to say, *Does she know you're a virgin, too?* But he couldn't. Not with Petros sitting in front.

'In fact, I shared the flat with her for a few months after college. But then—' She stopped. 'Well, stuff happened.'

He was intrigued. But Petros stopped him pursuing that one, too. Next time, Jay thought savagely, he was going to bring his own car.

Zoe leaned forward. 'Just here, on the left. Leave me on the corner, if you like. It's only a step.'

'I always see my dates indoors,' said Jay firmly.

'But I'm not—' She stopped, gave a quick look at the back of Petros's head, and subsided. 'Thank you,' she muttered.

Did she not want to sully his reputation for being irresistible? Jay was touched—and rather annoyed. He had been to a lot of parties with women like Susan Manoir. He knew what the men there were like. He did not want Zoe Brown to think of him as just another high-gloss stud, he found.

The chauffeur parked at the end of the street. Jay leaned forward and touched his shoulder.

'Wait. I may be a few minutes.'

'Sure thing.'

Jay walked Zoe to a solid redbrick Edwardian block. She brought out a key, turned to him with her hand out.

'Thank you for seeing me home.'

He ignored the hand. Instead he took the key from her. 'Inside the door.'

She raised her eyebrows. 'I'm not going to be mugged by a mad overnight cleaning lady. That sort of thing doesn't happen in apartment blocks with carpeted corridors.'

'It won't if you're not on your own,' he agreed. He unlocked the door and waved her in ahead of him. 'Go on.'

She hesitated a moment. Then shrugged. 'You have an over-developed sense of responsibility.'

'So Susan gives you a key,' he said as they got into the old brass-studded elevator.

'She keeps wanting me to move back in.'

He could ask now. 'Why did you move out in the first place? You obviously still get on well. Didn't like her boyfriends?'

Zoe looked startled. 'Of course not.'

'Well, then?'

The elevator arrived at Suze's floor. The ceiling lights were dimmed discreetly. They walked down thick-piled carpet. It was all very expensive and absolutely silent. They stopped at the door.

'Well?' persisted Jay.

Zoe rubbed her eyes tiredly. There was something about him that was implacable, somehow. She gave a deep sigh, stopped rubbing her eyes, and gave up her attempt at family discretion.

'There was trouble at home. My young brother was running wild. My mother needed reinforcements.'

She unlocked the door. It led straight into the main room. It was in total darkness, the furniture just ghostly shapes. From the kitchen there was the quiet hum of a fridge defrosting itself. Apart from that the place was silent.

Jay did not wait to be invited in. He pushed the door closed behind him and hunted down a table-lamp without much difficulty.

'Is Susan in?' he asked softly, switching it on.

'Don't expect so.'

Zoe slid off her strappy sandals and padded over the polished wooden floor into the internal corridor. She was back inside a minute.

'No. Her bedroom door's open and there's no one there. She's either still clubbing or she's gone off to meet Hermann somewhere. They were talking about Paris.'

'Good,' said Jay. He stopped whispering. 'You can give me a coffee and tell me the rest of this saga.'

Zoe was genuinely taken aback. 'You can't drink coffee at this hour.'

Jay grinned. 'Watch me.'

She shrugged. 'Fine, if that's what you want. But you'll never sleep.'

Jay's eyes gleamed. 'You don't know me well enough to say that.'

Something flickered in Zoe's stomach at the careless intimacy of that. It implied that she might—that she *could*—

She did not want to think about that. She flung up her hands. 'Okay. Okay. Your choice! Your nightmares! Just don't blame me.'

'I won't.'

She went into the small kitchen area and filled the kettle. Jay followed her, and sat down on one of the pine chairs at the table. He watched her rummage deep in the cupboard under the microwave until she found a small cafetière.

'You do know this place well, don't you?' he said thoughtfully.

Zoe straightened, reaching into the fridge for a packet of ground coffee. 'I live in hopes I'll move back one day,' she said unwarily.

'When you're no longer needed as reinforcement?'

'Yes.'

He nodded slowly. 'Your father is dead? Abroad? In prison?'

Zoe put down the foil pack so suddenly that coffee skittered across the pristine work surface like fingerprint powder. *'Prison?'*

'He's the natural reinforcement,' he pointed out. 'Not you. If he's not around, there has to be a really good reason.'

She gave a harsh choke of laughter. 'There is. She's called Saffron. Nearer my age than Mum's, with a heart like a calculator.'

Jay digested this in silence.

She shook her head. 'Damn. Why did I say that?'

Jay looked at her flushed face as she shovelled the spilt coffee into the cafetière with jerky movements. She seemed really furious with herself.

He said gently, 'Because you needed to, at a guess.'

Zoe put down coffee and cafetière, and stood back. She was looking at the mess on the work surface with something like horror. As he watched she put up both hands and pushed her hair back, pulling so tight he could see the pale skin stretching over he temples. Her hands were shaking.

'I don't know what's got into me tonight,' she said in a suffocated voice. 'I never say things like that. Mum always wants me to slag off Saffron and I won't.' She whipped round, hands on the work-top behind her, and glared at him. 'Did you put something in my drink?'

Jay raised his eyebrows. 'Oh, sure,' he said dryly. 'I always carry truth serum with me.'

At that, she smiled reluctantly. 'Sorry. Stupid of me. Just that tonight—'

'Yes,' he said softly. 'Tonight has been strange.'

If she had been sitting opposite him at the kitchen table he would have taken her hand then. But she wasn't. She was three feet away, staring at him as if she could not imagine how she had let him in here.

'Weird. I'd never have thought of having coffee with you after midnight in a million years.'

'Gee, thanks, Zoe. You're just great for the ego.'

She brushed aside his wounded ego without apology. 'Well, not like this, I mean.'

The thought flittered across his brain that he had never before sat across a kitchen table at four in the morning with a woman who worked for him. Still less asked her to tell him her life story. He dismissed it.

'So, what else do you need to get off your chest?' he said lightly. 'Lives at home. Doesn't want to. Dreams of getting away...'

'It's not like that—' she began. But then the kettle boiled and she had to concentrate on making the coffee.

Jay sniffed the rich air appreciatively. 'Kaldi, you're my man.'

Zoe looked up, confused. 'What?'

'Kaldi. Ethiopian shepherd. Supposed to have discovered coffee.'

'You mean it wasn't Sir Walter Raleigh?'

'Hey, English pirates didn't discover all the recreational drugs of choice,' he said, reaching for the cafetière.

Zoe searched a cupboard, failed to find mugs, and opened the dishwasher. She hooked out a couple of elegant black and gold mugs, sniffed them, decided they were clean, but ran them under the hot tap just to be certain.

'High housekeeping skills,' murmured Jay, entertained.

Zoe was practical. 'No, but I know Suze. I don't want to add salmonella to this evening's new experiences.'

She banged the mugs down on the table between them. He pressed the filter down through the coffee sludge. Zoe was turning back to the fridge, but for some reason she stopped, mesmerised. He was doing it very, very slowly. With relish, even. Her colour rose inexplicably.

'You look as if you've done that before.'

He gave her his wicked up-and-under look. 'My speciality.'

She swallowed. 'Yes. Well. Er—milk?'

He declined. Flustered, she spent a great deal longer than was necessary poking around in the fridge for juice. By the time she came up for air he had set a chair for her opposite him.

'So talk!' he commanded, taking the juice away from her.

She sank onto the chair, watching him pour first her juice then his coffee.

'That poor man outside in the car—'

'Believe me, he won't be complaining. The longer I stay out, the more he earns. At triple time,' Jay told her, amused. *'Talk.'*

She huffed a bit. 'I don't think I can,' she said candidly. 'I don't know how I came to tell you anything in the first place.

'So you said. I guess it's just timing. Look on me as your friendly neighbourhood busybody, if it helps. Pretend we're leaning on the back fence.'

She looked at him. He was devastatingly attractive, with his smooth dark hair faintly tumbled and those spectacular cheekbones.

Zoe's lips twitched. 'Oh, yes, I can just see the hairnet.'

'Hold that thought,' he said, unoffended. He drank some coffee. 'So run it past me again. You're twenty-three. Yet you still live at home. You look like a dream. Your friends all think you're a raver. You ought to be a raver. And yet you're a virgin.'

She stiffened. But his tone was so utterly dispassionate that all her defensiveness fell away from her. She bit her lip.

'Yes.'

'And,' said Jay shrewdly, 'you're not happy about it.'

Zoe winced.

His voice softened. 'Want to tell me why?'

'Well, like you said—everybody thinks I'm a raver.'

His brows twitched together. 'Don't understand.'

Zoe struggled to explain. 'I have friends. Good friends. They think they know everything there is to know about me. And I've got this big secret—'

She spread her hands eloquently. 'It's like I'm cheating. All the time.'

He shook his head, still bewildered. 'Cheating how?'

'Living a lie,' she said impatiently. 'And I've been doing it for *years*.'

'Ah. I think I begin to see.'

He swirled the coffee in his mug.

'Let's look at this another way. What was it that turned you off men? Something traumatic?'

Zoe sighed. 'There you go. That's why I've never told anyone. Nothing turned me off men,' she said impatiently. 'I'm not off men. Some of my best friends are men.'

'Well, then—'

'If I told Suze now, she'd think I'd suffered some big tragedy. Been beaten up or something. It's not true. No man's ever hurt me. No one's ever let me down. I just—never got round to sex.'

'Never got round to it?' Jay found he was speechless.

Defensiveness crept back. 'I was busy.'

'But what about all those men you know? Quite apart from your own hormones, what about the other side of the equation? They can't all have been busy, too?'

'Ah.' Zoe looked faintly uncomfortable. 'Well, you see, they all thought I'd got someone else.'

He shook his head. 'I can't get my head round this. How did they think you had someone else? How come you didn't have someone else?'

She shrugged. 'Our old friend timing, I suppose. My parents started to break up just as I was doing my first public exams. Then, when I was at university, I came home a lot because my brother and sister were still at school and—' She bit her lip. 'My mother went onto an alternative clock, making breakfast at midnight, that sort of thing. Someone had to keep the household fed and laundered.'

'Reinforcements,' he said, enlightened.

She flushed. 'If you like. Anyway, the boys at university all thought I had a boyfriend at home. And the boys at home—when I saw them—thought I had a boyfriend at college. So did my sister. And I always had plenty of friends who were men, sort of in the general crowd. So nobody noticed the difference.'

His eyebrows hit his hairline. 'But what about you?'

She looked surprised. 'I told you. I was busy.'

'Very few adolescent girls are so busy they fail to notice that they fancy the pants off the man of their dreams,' he said dryly.

She flushed deeper. 'Maybe I'm just cold hearted.'

'Do you think so?' he said ironically. 'Then what's all this about?'

He leaned forward and touched a gentle forefinger to the corner of her eye. It came away with a teardrop on the tip.

Zoe was horrified. She blinked rapidly.

'That just because I'm tired,' she said defiantly.

'And wound as tight as a spring about to break,' he agreed amiably.

She leaped up. 'No, I'm not. I'm nowhere near breaking point,' she said fiercely. 'Nowhere near. Do you hear me?'

He titled his chair back and looked at her ironically. 'Sure. That's why you're shouting, is it? So I can hear you?'

Zoe stopped dead, as if he had shot her.

She looked at his lounging body. Suddenly all the implications of the scene rose up and hit her in the face. This was a man who was so sexy his female staff e-mailed him love letters. They were alone in the flat while the stars glittered outside. She was young and attractive and unattached. What was more, she—in his phrase—fancied the pants off him.

And they were on opposite sides of the kitchen table while she shouted and he glared.

Suze would have been in his arms by now. It was too much! Any minute now she *was* going to cry, Zoe thought. She stumbled over to the counter and tore off a great wad of kitchen paper. She blew her nose loudly.

Jay got to his feet.

'Hey,' he said, touched. 'It's no big deal.'

'I'm *tired*,' said Zoe again loudly. She blew her nose harder.

He skirted the table and put an arm round her. She resisted for a moment. But he was strong and, heck, half of her wanted to feel what it was like to be in his arms anyway. She let him pull her against his body. It felt like a rock.

Or, no, like sun-warmed earth, solid and fertile. She buried her face in his shoulder for a moment. It did not feel natural—she stood awkwardly, all elbows and knees, and her feet were in the wrong place. But he did not seem to notice. And he smelled like heaven.

Only a moment, she promised herself. She rubbed her face against the linen jacket a little, savouring the scent of sandalwood with a deep underlying note of healthy male skin. She hoped the movement was unobtrusive. *Pathetic, or what?*

And if she was going to be that pathetic, she might as well go the whole hog.

'Okay,' she said into his jacket. 'So what do I do?'

Jay smiled. She could feel him smile, even with her face against his shoulders. Did he smile with his collarbone, for heaven's sake? How much did she not know about men's bodies that she had never realised?

'Back fence gossips don't give advice,' he said smugly.

He put his other arm round her. Purely for comfort, of course, thought Zoe. And she had been held lots of times. Kissed lots of times. Only somehow she had never felt so naked in a man's arms before. Crazy, when she was still dressed from head to toe. *But he knows more about me than anyone else in the world,* she thought.

It was a sobering thought. It brought her upright. Though it felt like death to leave that unemotional embrace.

She grabbed some more kitchen paper and blotted her eye make-up carefully.

'Sorry. That was stupid.' She sniffed. Then said in a stronger tone, 'You're not just a busybody. You're not my therapist.'

He frowned quickly. 'Heaven forfend.'

'So tell me like a friend.'

Jay was surprised. He hesitated for a moment. Then shrugged.

'Fine. If you want the truth, as a friend, I think you're making a fuss about nothing.'

Zoe took some time to assimilate that.

'So why doesn't it feel like nothing?'

'That's what interests me, too,' he said. She could feel him watching her. 'What does it feel like?'

'A bloody great mountain range with me on the wrong side of it,' she said explosively.

Jay's eyes narrowed. 'The unknown is always intimidating.'

'You don't understand,' said Zoe exasperated. 'It's not just that I haven't done it. It's that all my friends think I have.'

'So do it,' he said, bored.

'How?' she almost screamed.

'Tell one of all those men that there's a vacancy,' he advised. His eyes glittered like some particularly satanic polished stone. 'Does it really matter who?'

It did, but Zoe did not know why. Or how to explain it. Or how to defend her sentimentality from this super-sophisticate's derision. He probably saw this as a strictly practical problem. He would have no patience with her quivering vulnerability.

Get a grip, Zoe.

She muttered, 'Probably not, if it's happened thousands of time before. But first time—if you don't know your way around at my age, it's sort of embarrassing. I'm not a freak, and I'm not a victim of nameless tragedy.' She thought about it.

'Well, actually, yes, I am a freak, I suppose. But I'm not anti-sex. Just anti-embarrassment.'

There was a silence. Suddenly Zoe realised that the middle of the night was *cold*.

'If you really want my advice,' said Jay in a level voice, 'and strictly as a disinterested by-stander, I'd say find a stranger, do it once, and forget about it.'

She swallowed. 'That's easier said than done.'

'Oh, I don't know.' The hard voice sounded almost like an insult. As if he meant it to be an insult. 'What you need is something disposable. A lover to go.'

It hurt. Zoe did not know why, but it made her feel like a piece of trash. Boring trash, at that. Tears threatened again, shockingly. She bit down hard on her lower lip. She was not going to cry in front of Jay Christopher.

'Thank you for your advice,' she said coolly. 'I'll give it some serious thought. And now you really mustn't keep that poor driver waiting any more.'

She held out her hand again, firmly. This time he was not going to ignore it and talk his way into her confidence again.

But it seemed that this time he did not want to ignore it. He took her hand. Crushingly. Shook it twice, hard.

And then—

And then, he jerked her off balance and back into his hard arms. This time she had no time to think about elbows or feet or anything else. This time she had to concentrate on breathing.

It was a hard kiss. Not the sort of kiss you gave a girl who had just told you her most shameful secrets. Not a kiss you gave a girl you had made feel naked in your arms. Not a kind or gentle kiss at all.

'How can you?' choked Zoe, cut to the heart.

She hauled away from him, dashing her hand across her mouth as if she wanted to wipe away the memory of his touch. 'Why did you do that?' she said in despair.

He glittered down at her, his jaw rigid.

'Don't think you'll have a problem,' he drawled. He brushed his thumb across her lower lip, where it still throbbed. 'You can stop worrying about being cold. Not a chance.'

Zoe stood as if turned to stone. Jay waited a second or two, then gave a soft laugh.

He walked out before she could think of one single thing to say.

CHAPTER SEVEN

NEXT morning Jay went for a run. A long run on the Heath. He was furious with himself.

Why *had* he done that? Zoe was a member of his staff. Okay temporary. But that did not make any difference. He had his standards. Hell, he had sacked Barbara Lessiter for breaching them. And then, alone in the small hours with a woman he had known was tired to the point of exhaustion, he'd done exactly the same thing.

No, what he had done was worse. She had trusted him. And he'd betrayed that trust.

His feet pounded rhythmically on the rough grass. Later the sun would bake it dry, but at this hour of the morning he sent up little silver sparklers of dew with each footfall. Normally he would enjoy it. There were stages of his long-distance runs which were pure purgatory. But this piece of Heath, high and relatively flat, with the distant towers of the City shimmering in the dawn light, was balm to body and spirit. Usually.

Not this morning. He kept seeing Zoe scrubbing her hand across her mouth as if his kiss had contaminated her. And he lost focus.

A stitch knifed into him. Jay was used to running with pain. You just made your pace even, breathed regularly, and ran through it. In the end it went away. Not this morning.

He kept hearing himself say, 'What you need is…a lover to go.' He did not recognise the hard voice as his own. Yet he knew he had said it.

The pain intensified, as if someone was turning a stiletto in his side. He tried to breathe through it. It was no good. He stumbled. Nearly fell. Slowed to an uneven lurch.

Jay was enough of an expert to know that this was going to get him nowhere. He stopped dead, a hand to his side.

What was he going to do? Somehow he had to put it right. He wanted—no, he *needed*—to wipe out that look of betrayal. Zoe had such an expressive face, God help him.

He breathed with care until the pain subsided. Then he straightened slowly.

What was he thinking? What did it matter how expressive her face was? She was an employee. A temporary employee, sure. But still she worked for him. She could be as expressive as she liked. *It had nothing to do with him.*

And yet—he had not liked it when she'd first come to work for him and she had told him he'd never be a candidate. He went hot, remembering. No, he had not liked that at all. He had told himself it was all for the best. But he had called her in to his office every chance he had. Some of his excuses had been so thin he'd half expected her to challenge them, too.

Face it, Jay. You broke your own rules with Zoe Brown. And you did it long before she spilled out her secrets.

He was shaken. He did some stretches, carefully. Then he walked back to his house, frowning. He did not even try to break into a jog.

Okay, so he'd broken his own rules. Well, he would pay his own price. He would keep out of the office as much as possible. Certainly he would keep away from Zoe. When her contract was up—well, then he could think again. But until then he would just give her some space.

It cost him restless days and sleepless nights. He snapped at everyone. He jumped every time his mobile phone rang. He got a mountain of work done. And he bit the head off anyone who asked him what was wrong.

He scanned his e-mail hourly for messages from her. But when they came they were only about the Venice speech.

On Friday morning he gave up and went in to the office. He told himself it was to pick up the material he would need for the seminar. But he knew perfectly well that Poppy could have had the stuff biked round to his Hampstead house if he'd wanted. He didn't. He wanted the chance—just the chance—of seeing Zoe.

And his gamble paid off. Almost as soon as he was in the building, he saw her coming down the silver staircase with Abby and Molly di Paretti. The other two smiled broadly but Zoe would not meet his eyes. In fact she dodged round Molly and disappeared, while the Fab Ab buttonholed him.

'You've got a new wall ornament,' she said.

Jay was looking after Zoe's retreating figure. 'What?'

'The London Youth Clubs have sent you a presentation baseball bat,' said Abby. 'Along with an invitation to run in their All-Time Greats event in September.'

Jay wanted to follow Zoe so badly that it hurt. 'Why are you telling me this?'

Abby looked surprised. 'The Youth Club is my account. You gave it to me. I think it would be great if you did the run.'

'You know I don't compete any more,' he snarled. He took a step towards the door, in the direction that the girls had taken.

Abby took hold of his arm and made him face her. 'And I need to talk to you about the PR for *Lemon Sherbet Three*. The film company is having a row with the UK distributors.'

Jay gave up. 'We'll have a round up meeting at midday,' he said, resigned. 'Tell me then.'

She nodded. 'Boardroom. Noon. Got it.'

She sped away. As she got to the door he called, 'Ab—'

She turned warily. 'Yes?'

'Sorry I snapped.'

She gave him a kind smile. 'Don't worry about it. We all have off days.'

But when she got to Patisserie Patricia her smile had died.

'If you ask me, the Volcano is going to blow,' she said, sinking down behind a tall glass of iced coffee. 'Is that why you didn't want to talk to him, Zoe?'

Zoe seized the excuse thankfully. 'He's been getting mad at me. This Venice talk.'

'But you've done such a good job on getting all the material together,' said Abby, indignant. 'You really saved his bacon. It's not like Jay to ignore that. Is it, Molly? He's always really nice if you do a good piece of work.'

Molly said slowly, 'I've never seen him like this.'

'Too right,' said Abby with feeling. 'I thought I wasn't going to hold him off for you, Zoe. There was one point he looked like he was going to pick me up and put me out of the way.'

Zoe did not meet their eyes. 'The Venice talk must be getting to him.'

'Garbage,' said Molly. 'He gives talks all the time.'

'Yes, but I don't think he's even started on it yet,' Zoe said earnestly. 'And he's supposed to deliver it on Monday.'

'That would do it for me,' agreed Abby.

Molly said nothing. But she narrowed her eyes in a way that made Zoe feel guilty. She did it again when later a summons came from Jay's blonde PA.

'He wants to talk to you, Zoe,' Molly said, putting the phone down. 'Better get up there now.'

Zoe went white.

Molly picked up the pile of cuttings and prints-offs in her pending tray and slapped them into her arms. 'He probably wants you to do a first draft of his speech,' she said with emphasis. 'God knows, you've done everything else.'

Everything else? Zoe stared at her in wild suspicion. Were her feelings for Jay Christopher written all over her face, for heaven's sake?

'Keep your head down and don't say more than you have to,' Molly advised, oblivious. 'Good luck.'

The advice was unnecessary. As soon as Zoe came face to face with Jay across his impressive desk she was absolutely tongue-tied.

Where was Performance Zoe when you needed her? she thought in despair.

Jay seemed to be preoccupied. He waved her into a seat and concentrated on the papers in front of him for what felt like hours. It was intimidating. It occurred to her that it was meant to be intimidating, and her sense of justice reasserted itself. After all, she was not the one who had laid hands on him first.

Zoe glared at the top of his head and began to feel a bit better.

She said acidly, 'Am I going to sit here all day, or would you like me to come back when you've finished the crossword puzzle?'

Jay looked up at that, though he did not meet her eyes. He said abruptly, 'I owe you an apology.'

Zoe stared. 'What?'

'The last time we met I kissed you. I knew you didn't want it and I kissed you anyway. I had no right to do that. I'm sorry.'

It was what she had been saying to herself all week. *He had no right!* And now that he'd come right out and apologised she felt—well, cheated.

'Guys don't normally apologise for kissing me.'

'I'm not a guy; I'm your employer. It was—inappropriate.'

'You know, you can sound so stuffy sometimes.'

He smiled faintly. 'Stuffy, maybe. It's still the truth. You work for me. That puts you off-limits. I shouldn't have forgotten that.'

Zoe found her anger had evaporated. It was rather a lonely feeling. She had been talking to that anger all week.

She said sadly, 'I suppose I was inappropriate, too. Telling you all that about—'

'It didn't help,' agreed Jay. 'Turned up the volume on intimacy, I suppose you could say.'

She shook her head. 'It may have felt like that to you. To me, it was like spilling everything out to one of those late-night phone-in programmes on the radio.'

'A faceless voice in the dark? Gee, thanks.'

'Well, not faceless, maybe. But remote. And—'

'No come-back,' said Jay slowly. 'I'm strictly disposable in your life, aren't I?'

Did he sound hurt? Zoe could not believe it. Yet somehow she felt ashamed. As if she had stamped on his feelings in pursuit of her own need to unload. She bit her lip.

'I think it was more that we had no history,' she said honestly.

He looked at her for a long moment. The heavy-lidded eyes were quite inscrutable. Then he leaned back in his chair.

'Explain,' he invited.

'You see, all my friends know me very well. If they find out I've been keeping this huge secret they will either not believe me or feel cheated. Maybe even both.'

'A stranger is safe because you have nothing to lose?' he said on a note of discovery.

'I suppose so.' She sounded subdued, even to her own ears. She rallied, trying to make a joke out of it. 'I guess I wanted you to turn into a psychiatrist and tell me what to do.'

He stared at her for a long minute, unblinking. 'I didn't think psychiatrists were supposed to give advice.'

'So what do they do?'

'Listen, I gather. Ask the right questions, hopefully.'

For some reason Zoe was outraged. She snorted. 'Money for old rope,' she muttered.

His mouth tilted suddenly. 'That sounds a bit harsh.'

Zoe waved that aside. Suddenly she was urgent. 'Okay. Forget the radio psychiatrist. What would you have said to me if I'd told you that as a friend?'

He raised his eyebrows. 'You mean, imagine we have a history?'

'Yes.'

He pondered. She saw him reach a conclusion. He hesitated for a moment. Then shrugged.

'Fine. I told you that night, if you remember. I gave you the full benefit of my considered advice then. You didn't,' he added with point, 'seem to appreciate it.'

She flushed. 'You said I was making a fuss about nothing.'

He had also said, *'Find a stranger, do it once and forget about it.'* But she wasn't going to think about that just now.

'I might have been harsh,' Jay allowed. He surveyed her watchfully. 'I think you have to ask yourself why you are making such a fuss. There's nothing to be ashamed of, after all. We all start out virgins.'

Zoe gave a startled little spurt of laughter, as if he had said something genuinely shocking.

'I never thought of that.'

'Well, hang on to it,' he advised.

'Yes, but—'

'And it doesn't matter what your friends think.'

'It matters what I think, though. And I think I'm a fraud.'

She had never said it so baldly, not even to herself. She fell silent, feeling sick.

Jay's expression told her nothing. He studied her as if she were an interesting specimen page for a long minute.

Then he said, 'Maybe you didn't go to bed with anyone because you weren't in love.'

'In love?' She snorted with derision. 'Now you're really thinking I'm nuts.'

'It is just conceivable.'

'No, it isn't.'

His eyes glinted. 'Many people think being in love is indispensable.'

Was he laughing at her? Zoe's chin came up and she glared at him, eye to eye.

'That didn't stop any of my friends,' she said deliberately. 'Did it stop you?'

His expression did not change. But somehow she knew that she had struck home. She could feel his withdrawal, though physically he did not move a muscle. The elegant body still lounged there as casually as if they were old, old friends who bared their souls to each other all the time.

'No,' he said at last. His lips barely moved. His voice was light, level. 'No, lack of love didn't stop me. Maybe it should have.'

Zoe looked ironic. 'Don't do as I do, do as I say? Thanks for the insight.'

He looked irritated. 'Look, this is no big deal. It's a just a physical thing you go through. Like—like the pain barrier when you're running. It's not the reason you do it, but it happens. You get through it.'

'Wow, sounds irresistible. Come to bed with me and I'll get through it.'

Jay grinned. But he said, 'I think you're looking at this the wrong way. For some men it would be a great compliment.'

'Yeah. The sad sickos who see virginity as a trophy. Like I'm going to do a deal with one of them.'

'We're not all like that. There are men for whom it would be—' he struggled to put his feeling into words '—a great sign of trust. Respect. Even love.'

Zoe looked at him oddly. 'Oh, yeah? Respect, huh? Do your girlfriends respect you?'

He stiffened. 'I hope so.'

'And how many of them have been virgins?'

'None, as far as I know.' He thought about it, and added involuntarily, 'God, I hope not. No, I'm sure not. I've never been—' He stopped.

'A sad sicko who sees it as a trophy?' supplied Zoe, half-weary, half-triumphant. 'See what I mean? Catch Twenty-two.'

He got up and began to move restlessly round the room. 'I don't believe it. There has to be a solution.'

'If there was, don't you think I'd have found it?' flashed Zoe. 'I've been pretending like this for five years. Ever since I was the last eighteen-year-old virgin in Muswell Hill. Short of a miracle, I'm stuck like this for life.'

He looked at her—the crop top, the slim thighs, the clear skin and clearer eyes—and said from the heart, 'That's ludicrous.'

'Yeah? You think so? Well, let me tell you it isn't. It's like the old Marx Brothers thing. I don't want to be a member of any club that would accept me. Any guy who is into deflowering virgins is someone I want to avoid like the plague.'

Jay said impatiently, 'So don't tell him.'

'Oh, great. That's a real sign of trust.'

He was getting annoyed. 'So there's no easy answer. How like life. There's going to be a tough answer somewhere, though. Go look for it.'

Zoe said with spurious affability, 'Do you know you do that all the time?'

'Do what?'

'Patronise me. We get into an argument and you're soon losing it. So you patronise me. The next time you do it I'll take that baseball bat off your wall and brain you with it. I swear I will.'

'You could always try sounder arguments,' he said lightly.

But Zoe had gone beyond the possibility of laughter. She jumped to her feet glaring.

'There you go again. Don't you dare patronise me ever again, you—you—you *spin doctor*.'

Jay blinked. 'Is that mean to be an insult?'

'Too right.'

He turned on her, his eyes glittering dangerously. 'Then let me tell you, I am very good at what I do.'

'Sure. Probably the best there is,' said Zoe viciously. 'Doesn't mean it's worth doing.'

He stopped pacing as if she had thrust a fist straight into his heart. 'At least I'm doing something,' he said very quietly. 'Not whingeing that life shouldn't be as it is.'

Her eyes widened in shock.

'Yes, you can hand it out, can't you?' said Jay, still in that same deadly quiet voice. 'You're allowed no holds barred, a pretty young thing like you. Doesn't matter who you hurt. God, I'm so tired of noisy women who don't give a stuff about anything except their own petty neuroses.'

Zoe was very pale. 'I'm sorry you think it's petty. I suppose in comparison with publicising *Lemon Sherbet Three* it must lack a certain global significance.'

Jay winced. 'I didn't mean that.'

She ignored him, going to the door a little blindly. 'But, as I keep trying to tell you—it's not a neurosis. It's a question of ethics.'

He snorted. 'Ethics, schmethics. It's a practical problem, pure and simple. All you need is a bit of courage to sort it out.'

She turned and met his eyes.

'Okay. Here's a solution. You know all there is to know about sex and you're not into trophies. You do it.'

They stared at each other. Equally appalled at what she had said. Equally silent.

Zoe was the first to break eye contact. Her smile was twisted.

'See? That's not just a practical problem. Is it?'

And she walked out.

Jay did not want to go to the reception. It would be full of media types, networking. Besides, he did not have time. He was off to Venice tomorrow, and he had not begun to think of what to tell the international public relations consultants who were coming from five continents to hear his great thoughts. He was desperate for some time to himself.

But his host was thinking of commissioning a television programme about youth athletics, and Jay was chair of the committee that was lobbying hard. Maybe tonight would clinch it. So he briefed himself on the latest figures on training facilities, inner-city population and youth crime, climbed into a formal dinner jacket—and went.

He did not manage to catch sight of Zoe Brown on his way out of the building. He supposed she had already left for the weekend. He wondered how she spent her free time. And with whom.

His hands clenched at the thought. Damn, that was not sensible. He could not afford to think things like that, not while she still worked for him.

He stamped into the reception looking like a conquering emperor in a seriously bad temper. And the moment he walked in the first person he saw was Carla.

She was looking very beautiful. He would have to talk to her, Jay knew. He curbed his temper ruthlessly. It was more difficult than he would have believed possible.

She was wearing cream silk, very plain, with the watery aquamarines he had given her in her ears and at her throat. Bless her heart, she smiled with unaffected pleasure when she caught sight of him in the doorway. The frustrated temper eased a little. When she made her way over to him he even managed a decent smile.

'Hi, Carla. You're looking very glam.'

'Thank you, Jay. How are you?'

'Fine. You?'

'Better every day,' she told him gaily.

He looked at her searchingly. 'Is that true?'

Her eyebrows flew up. 'What's happened to you, then?'

Jay was confused. 'What?'

'You don't ask uncomfortable questions like that.'

'What do you mean?'

'Well, for one thing it's not polite. For another, you don't want to know the answers.'

He blinked.

Carla smiled, putting an exquisitely manicured hand on his arm. 'Jay, we were an item for six months. In all that time I told you a lot of comfortable platitudes. You never questioned them once. So what's with the tell-me-the-truth game?'

He said slowly, 'I hurt you a lot, didn't I?'

Carla shook her head, smiling steadily. 'You're a fun date and a terrific lay. And you never make promises you can't keep. I had my six months of fantasy. My friends envy me.'

Jay was shaken. He said to the look in her eyes, 'I never realised—'

'I did,' said Carla, suddenly curt. 'My risk. My choice. And it was worth it. Don't you dare be sorry for me.'

The party seethed around them. He said in a rapid under-voice, 'Can I give you dinner after this? Can we talk?'

'No.'

He was taken aback.

She looked past his shoulder, the smile firmly in place. 'I've moved on, Jay. From the sound of it, you're doing the same thing.'

'What?'

'Going back is no solution. We may not be too happy at the moment. But we'll come through that.'

Someone was coming over, going to join them. She took her hand off his arm. The smile she gave him was wide and friendly. And if her eyes were a bit too bright, well, no one but Jay would have noticed. Jay, after all, had looked into her eyes, up close, a thousand times.

He felt like a heel. The worst heel in the world. *This woman slept in my arms and I didn't take care of her.*

Carla shook her head at the look in his eyes. 'The past is great compost, Jay. Leave it to do its work.'

She turned to the new arrival, delighted, made introductions, and then drifted away. He did not see her again.

He had not intended to drink, so he had taken his own car. He sat in it, the top down, savouring the night air, trying to wrestle his thoughts into coherence.

He could not. All he could think of was what he had done to Carla. And, almost worse somehow, how Zoe had looked when she'd walked away from him today.

Is there no end to the damage I do?

He made up his mind.

The roads were nearly empty at this time of night. He had a brief flicker of unease about turning up on her doorstep unannounced. But he did not have a phone number for her. He had never had to call her. He would just have to take a chance that she was in—and willing to open the door to him.

Zoe was doing the week's ironing. She liked ironing normally. She used it to work out her problems. It was mindless and soothing. Besides, everything ended up looking wonderful and smelling better.

But tonight, for some reason, it wasn't working. She burned a tee shirt she needn't have tried to iron. And then the catch on the ironing board didn't engage properly and when she pressed on a particularly dense bit of quilted jacket the board collapsed. She saved the iron and kicked the jacket clear. But she ended up sitting on the floor with a nasty burn on her arm, where she had not quite fielded the iron fast enough.

She felt very cold and shaky. She recognised it. Shock.

'Or another petty feminine neurosis,' she said aloud bitterly.

She had been trying to whip up indignation against Jay all evening. It was surprisingly difficult. The sneaking suspicion that he was right kept flitting across the back of her mind. Well, a bit right. Maybe.

She leaned sideways and pulled out the plug of the iron. Then she set it carefully on its end, in the corner. Her hands were shaking. Shock, definitely. Low-grade but still shock.

'Hot sweet tea,' she said aloud. 'Run cold water on the burn.'

She wished her mother would come down and help her. Deborah must have heard the crash of the falling ironing board, surely?

But she knew it was hopeless. If Deborah heard the crash she would just assume it was nothing to do with her and carry on watching her movie.

Face it, Zoe, you get yourself up or you stay sitting on the carpet for ever.

Zoe stood up carefully. Her arm throbbed and her legs were weak as water. But she was not hurt.

'I can do this,' she said, hanging on to the kitchen table.

It seemed like one of Jay's five-thousand-metre runs to get to the cold tap.

That was when the doorbell rang.

'Damn,' said Zoe with real feeling.

She considered not answering. It was past eleven, after all.

But anyone who rang the doorbell at past eleven was serious. Maybe Harry had decided he couldn't hack leading eleven-year-olds through salt flats, after all. Maybe he had dived for home and lost his key again. Clinging to the furniture, she made her way through the house and opened the front door.

And stared, open-mouthed.

It was Jay Christopher. Jay Christopher in a dinner jacket. His mouth was pinched as if he were in pain. But his jaw was determined.

'I'll do it,' he said.

Zoe put a hand against the doorframe to steady herself. Her legs still felt as if they were made of lint and her head was beginning to swim. Her burned arm throbbed, too. She had not the slightest idea what he was talking about.

'Sorry?'

'I've been thinking about it and I've decided. I'll—' Jay broke off suddenly. He leaned forward, his eyes growing intent. 'What's wrong?'

'N-nothing.'

'Yes, there is. You're shivering.'

She was, too. Although the summer night was almost as warm as the day.

He said sharply, 'What has happened?'

'It's nothing. I knocked over the ironing board, that's all. I burnt myself. Nobody heard—'

Zoe was in tears, mortifyingly. Neurosis, indeed! She turned away, trying to hide it from him.

But Jay pushed into the house and put his hands on her shoulders, turning her back. His sleeve brushed the burn on her arm and she yelped. At once he held her away from him, eyes narrowing as he saw the mark.

Shivering even harder, she said, 'It's not serious. I just need to run it under cold water.'

'Then let's do that,' said Jay calmly. He kicked the door closed without even looking at it. 'Kitchen is this way, right?'

She leaned as heavily against him as if she were a convalescent. He got her into the kitchen, took a chair to the sink and made her sit down. Then he held her arm under the cool stream of water.

'Feel faint?'

She smiled wanly. 'A bit.'

'Keep your head down. It will pass. I'll just check on the iron.'

She did what he said. It seemed easier. Besides, she was grateful. It was a long time since anyone had taken care of her. It was worth putting up with a bit of bossing.

He came back. 'The iron's cold. You did all the right things. Good girl.'

He put a cool hand to her forehead. It felt almost professional. Certainly quite without feeling. So Zoe was horrified to find that she wanted to lean against him and say, Hold me.

She cleared her throat. 'Thank you,' she said huskily.

Jay was wearing his hidden laughter look. His eyes glinted down at her.

'For what? Calling you a good girl? I thought you'd take a baseball bat to me if I patronised you again.'

She gave a watery chuckle. 'Thank you for not saying one word about neurotic women and their petty crises.'

'A burn is hardly neurotic.' He leaned over her shoulder to look at it. She felt the warmth of his body under the dark jacket, the strength…

Her mind flipped sideways. Try, it said.

What?

What have you got to lose? it said.

What do you mean?

Lean against him and see what he does. You know you want to.

I can't—

He's right. You're a coward.

Jay looked down at her. 'Hey, you're shaking again,' he said in concern. He slipped off his jacket and put it round her. 'That will have to do for the moment. I'm making you some tea. Then you can tell me where I find a blanket to put round you.'

Zoe moistened her lips. She was deeply, darkly ashamed of her secret thoughts.

'So much fuss for a little burn,' she said with constraint. 'I'll be fine. Just give me a minute. Though tea would be nice.'

Tea would get him away from her, over to the other side of the kitchen to make it. And maybe she would start to think clearly again.

Maybe she would have, if it had not been for that jacket. She rubbed her cheek against its comforting warmth. And smelled soap and the sea and some woody aromatic, not pine or sandalwood, but something like both, only more elusive. And a lot more exotic. Whatever it was, it was a clean, clear smell; sharp as a knife and utterly like Jay. Her senses swam.

I want him.

She jumped as if she had just impaled herself on a blackberry thorn.

I've wanted him since I first saw him. Since I told him everything there was to know about me. Since he kissed me.

'Do you take sugar?' said Jay, oblivious.

Zoe tried to speak. It was not easy. 'No,' she croaked on her third attempt.

'Well, I'm putting some in. It's supposed to be good for shock.'

How come it's taken me this long to realise? What sort of freak am I?

And her thoughts began to spiral faster and faster, out of control.

Jay came back with the tea. He had put it in the horrible dragon mug. 'Here. This will make you feel better.'

Zoe looked up at him dumbly. Her mind was still in free fall.

He smiled down at her, his face so gentle that she almost did not recognise him. He took both her hands and clasped them round the mug. Her fingers twitched but she took the mug. In fact she clutched it like a lifeline.

'Are you alone in the house?' he asked.

Zoe shook her head. 'My mother's in her room. She—er—can't have heard.'

He looked at the devastated ironing board. It had lost half its mechanism and brought down the clothes horse in its collapse. It was self-evident that it must have sounded like a falling tree in the confined space. Jay raised his eyebrows. But he refrained from comment.

'Just as well I arrived when I did, then.'

Even in the face of his courteous disbelief she still wanted him. Her hands were clammy with it.

Zoe swallowed. 'Yes.'

She had never felt like this before. Never felt a need to touch a man so fierce it seemed a physical impossibility not to give in to it. She clutched the mug so hard that her knuckles went white. She tried to collect her thoughts.

'What was it that you came for?' she said distractedly.

'Ah.'

Something in his voice—or not in his voice, in his eyes, in the way he was looking at her, though she had her head bent and could not even see him out of the corner of her eye, but she knew he was looking at her—*something* told her that this was not easy for him. Important, yes. Very important. But not easy. In fact, hard as hell.

She looked up, surprised. 'Yes?'

He cleared his throat. 'I've been thinking about your—er—solution. To the problem you think you have.'

She frowned, bewildered.

The wonderful golden skin did not flush, but his eyes slid away from hers.

'You were right. I was being glib. You have got more than a practical problem.'

'Oh!' Zoe's skin, however, flushed instantly and unmistakably.

'And you were right about something else. I'm not into trophies. But I do have all the relevant qualifications.' His voice was level.

'What?'

'I have it on the best authority,' said Jay in a hard voice, 'that I am a fun date and a terrific lay.'

It was somehow terrible. He looked as if someone had cut his heart out, thought Zoe. Whoever she was, the woman who'd told him that had devastated him. Suddenly Zoe wanted to take him in her arms and tell him it was a lie.

But she had no right. And besides—maybe it wasn't a lie. She huddled his embracing jacket round her and couldn't think of one single thing to say.

It did not matter. Jay was laying out his argument like a presentation to a client, all common sense and shining reason.

'You don't want to lie. You don't want to be a trophy. You need a man to help you through the transition. I can do that.'

'Oh,' said Zoe. She felt as if she were in a falling elevator. No solid ground anywhere and a distinct rushing sound in her ears.

'In fact I'm probably uniquely qualified to do that,' said Jay, bitterness seeping out. 'Mr No Commitment.'

'I—see.'

He leaned against a cupboard and looked all the way across the kitchen at her. Zoe shivered. His expression was brooding.

'No claims. No promises. No history. I'm the dream ticket, aren't I?'

Oh, you are! You are!

'I-er—I hadn't really thought about it,' said Zoe.

She was not certain if that was true. Certainly when she'd flung her challenge at him she had never thought for a moment that he would pick it up. Okay, this evening she had been shivering with desire just to touch him. But she was hurt and in shock. Surely anyone could be allowed a little fantasy at moments like that?

Except—where did it come from, that sensitivity to his touch, his voice, his glance, even the scents of his damned clothes?

Jay's voice gentled. 'Think about it now.'

She did. It brought an image of his hands on her, so clear that she broke out in a sweat. The elevator reversed polarity and took off like a rocket.

She said in a gasping voice, 'You really wouldn't mind?'

He laughed. 'You sound like a polite child. There's no need to be grateful. It's no hardship. You must know that you're gorgeous.'

He paused expectantly. Zoe did not say anything. Her head was so light she felt that she was curving round Mars with a comet tail of fire blazing after her.

'You know me. I'm not a good man. There are women I have hurt. But I can do this thing.' And, as she still said nothing, he added, 'Only if it will help, of course.'

Zoe, her ears ringing, was heading out of the solar system by now. She managed to gasp, 'Oh, it will. It will. I accept.'

That was when her numbed fingers lost their grip. The hated dragon mug crashed onto the tiled floor and broke into a thousand pieces. The shards scattered, powdering the floor and her discarded footwear. A great jagged piece with teeth lodged in her tumbled left shoe.

And Zoe, who loathed the dragons and all they represented, broke into inconsolable tears.

CHAPTER EIGHT

JAY was surprisingly competent with her tears. After a brief moment of pure, masculine horror, he picked her off the chair and crunched through the broken pottery to the French window. Hesitating only a moment with the handle, he shouldered his way out onto the night-time patio. There he dropped her onto the old wooden bench.

'Put my jacket on properly, or you'll get cold.'

Zoe sniffed.

He gave an exasperated sigh and whipped a pristine handkerchief out of his trouser pocket, stuffing it into her right hand. Then he took her left hand and inserted it into the left sleeve of the jacket and pushed.

Zoe blew her nose.

Gosh, I'm being pathetic, she castigated herself. But it felt wonderful to be so close to him, having him care for her. She let herself flop about like an awkward kindergarten pupil as he hauled. It gave her the chance to lean against him. Even—briefly—bury her nose in his crisp shirt-front. Heart-stopping!

Pull yourself together. You're not four years old.

Well, she had not been behaving in a very grown-up way since he'd arrived. But the way she felt in his arms was certainly not child-like. Time to take a hold on life again!

Zoe straightened, reluctant to leave his arms, knowing that she had to. 'It's all right. I've got it.'

At once, he stepped back.

Zoe tried not to feel bereft. She dealt with the other sleeve herself. The jacket was much too big, yet it felt as if she belonged in it. The lining slipped along her bare arms like a secret kiss. The way the lining moved against her skin, it had to be silk. Soft as a kiss but warm as a blanket, she thought, savouring the sensation. She gave a small, voluptuous shiver.

Jay said in a worried voice, 'You shouldn't be that cold. It's a warm night.'

'No—it's—I'm fine,' she said hurriedly. 'Thank you.'

He still looked down at her, frowning. 'Maybe that burn is worse than it looks. How does it feel now?'

She had almost forgotten the burn. She shook her head. 'Fine, honestly. The cold water has taken all the heat out of it.'

He was still doubtful. But he said, 'Stay there,' and went back into the house.

He came back with her shoes. He had clearly shaken all the shards of pottery out and, by the look of it, run them under the tap for good measure. They were certainly shiny, and slightly damp, inside and out, as well. He also had a worn piece of tartan cloth over his arm.

'All I could find,' he said briefly, offering it to her.

Zoe was pulling on her shoes. She looked up, shaking her head, laughing. 'It's the cat's blanket. Cyrus won't take it very kindly if I pinch it.'

'But—'

She straightened. 'Don't worry. I'm all right now. Truly. And I've got a kitchen floor to clean up. That will get the blood moving.'

'I'll get you some more tea first,' Jay said decisively. 'Then we'll see,'

He was as quick and efficient at that as he was at everything else. He brought it out to her and sat on the old chair opposite as she sipped. He leaned forward, looking at her keenly in the moonlight.

Zoe said uncomfortably, 'You're doing all the right things.'

He gave a ghost of laugh. 'Am I?'

She was flustered. 'I mean the treatment for superficial burns, shock—everything. Very professional.'

He sat back, shrugging. 'I've run training weekends for kids. I thought it was a good idea to learn basic first aid.'

She was glad that he did not seem to be studying her under a microscope any more. 'I would have thought that was just strained muscles and stuff. I mean running isn't exactly a high-risk sport. Is it?'

She saw the flash of white teeth as he grinned in the darkness.

'You have no idea what eleven-year-olds can do to themselves if they put their mind to it. If you ever get yourself stuck down a pot hole, I could probably get you out of that, too.'

'A pot hole?' gasped Zoe.

He smiled reminiscently. 'A little anarchist called Brian. Good runner, too. Just never got the idea of doing what he was told.'

Zoe made a discovery.

'You liked him.'

'I suppose I did.' He sounded surprised. 'He kept going off on his own all the time. I could identify with that.'

'You?' She was sceptical.

'Oh, yes. There's a lot more to me than a spin doctor who lights a trail to land third-rate movies, you know.'

She flushed in the dark. 'Sorry about that.'

'No need. I had it coming.'

'Even so—it wasn't fair. I didn't know you well enough to say a thing like that.'

He gave a soft laugh. 'No?'

She was oddly shocked. 'Of course not. A couple of conversations and a lot of gossip don't add up to knowing someone.'

'So why do I feel that you've known me since the first moment you looked through me?' Jay asked quietly.

'What?'

'Why do you think I was upset when you tweaked me about *Lemon Sherbet Three*?'

'I didn't know you were,' said Zoe, shaken.

'Oh, I was. And not because I expect the staff to sign up to my Napoleon image, either. I was upset because I thought—she could be right.'

'But—'

'You see clearly, Zoe Brown. I was worried that you were seeing through my protective colouring. And seeing how thin it was.'

She stared at him blankly.

'No!'

She saw one eyebrow lift. 'No? So what did you think of me?'

She shifted uncomfortably. 'I just thought you were—very busy.'

His expression was wry. 'You thought a lot more than that.'

He did not throw, *'You could never be a candidate,'* in her face, but he was tempted. Only it was not very chivalrous, when she was so shaken. And he was supposed to be here as her knight in shining armour.

He said, 'It's okay. You don't have to answer that.'

Zoe shook her head. 'No, it's a fair enough question. If you really want to know—I was surprised that you were so good at your job.'

Jay stared. It was the last thing he'd expected.

Zoe said thoughtfully, 'After all, you're hardly a people person, are you? I've watched you. Sometimes you look as if you've overdosed on humanity and are just desperate to get away from all of us.'

Jay went very still. 'You do know me, don't you?' he said, almost inaudibly.

Zoe was pursuing her own line of thought. 'You do what you have to. But people have to stand in line. Nobody gets more than their ration out of you.'

His head went back as if she had struck him. There was a turbulent silence.

He said at last ruefully, 'Ouch. You know how to hit where it hurts, don't you?'

Zoe was confused. 'I didn't mean—I was only saying what I felt. You asked,' she ended with a touch of indignation.

'I did. I did indeed. I can see I shall have to think before I ask in future.'

Zoe peered at him in the darkness. He sounded amused. But he also sounded as if it were a bit of an effort.

'Sorry,' she said, conscience-stricken.

Jay stuffed his hands in the pockets of his formal black trousers and looked up at the fingerprint moon.

'Probably good for me,' he said dispassionately. 'I've suspected for some time that people walk round me a bit too carefully. Never get to be the boss, Zoe. It changes things.'

He sounded half-sad, half-angry. Not angry with her, though, she thought. She hoped. She could not bear it if her thoughtless words had really hurt him.

He drew a long breath. Then said in quite a different tone, 'Now—to practicalities.'

At once Zoe stopped palpitating over his possible feelings and bounced right back into the present. She sat bolt upright.

'What—now?' she said, in stark horror.

Jay laughed aloud. 'Get real. We have a journey to go on first.'

She liked that 'we'. She relaxed. 'Thank heaven,' she said unwarily.

He stuffed his hands deeper in his pockets. 'And the first thing we need is neutral territory,' he said, as calmly as if he were discussing a PR campaign. 'You'd better come with me to Venice.'

Zoe spluttered.

'What have you got against Venice?' he said patiently.

'Nothing. I mean, I've never been. But I haven't got a ticket. And it's so *soon*.'

'I'll get you a ticket.' Jay was calm. 'And the sooner the better.'

'Oh,' said Zoe hollowly.

He took his hands out of his pockets and came over to her. Zoe tensed in the darkness. But he just buffed her cheek lightly.

'Believe me.' His voice was kind. 'Once you've made up your mind to do something you don't want to, the best thing is to get it over with.'

'Oh,' she said again in quite a different voice.

She felt cold suddenly. It had nothing to do with the summer night air. She huddled his jacket round her, and the scents of his skin assaulted her like a reproach.

'This is very kind of you,' she said with constraint.

He did not answer that. He was thinking. 'I'll send a car to pick you up tomorrow. About eleven. Bring a business suit for Monday, and some walking shoes so we can do the ritual sightseeing.'

Her heart fluttered madly. *I don't believe I'm doing this.*

'All right,' she said aloud.

He touched her cheek again. 'You'll be back Monday night. Then you can get on with the rest of your life.'

She swallowed. Monday night! After two days in uncharted territory, who could guess where she would be going by then?

Get a grip, Zoe. Get a grip.

She stood up. 'That will be great,' she said distractedly, as if he had just offered her a job, or a ride to the station on a wet morning. 'I'd better tell my mother. And clear up the mess in the kitchen. Um—your jacket.'

She struggled out of it and handed it across. He hooked a finger into the tab at the collar and swung it over his shoulder.

As they went into the house he put a brotherly arm round her. Zoe was sure it was meant to be brotherly. But it made her quiver from her breastbone to her toes. She moved away from him and speeded up.

'Goodnight,' she said, opening the front door with indecent haste. 'I'll see you tomorrow.'

Jay was not dismissed so easily. He leaned one arm against the lintel and looked down at her very seriously.

'Only if you want to. Never forget, this is your idea. Any time you want to back out, you just say so.'

She wanted him to kiss her so much she almost pulled him into her arms. Almost. What stopped her was the thought that the kiss would probably be kind and brotherly. She did not think she could bear that.

'I'll keep that in mind,' she promised brightly. 'Goodnight.'

She had the door closed on him before he was down the path to the gate.

One good thing about being in a flat panic about a man was that it put everything else into a new perspective, thought Zoe. Last week she would have prepared her mother so carefully, filled the fridge with food, alerted the neighbours. Now she just went into Deborah's room, as soon as he had gone, and laid her cards on the table.

'I'm going to Venice tomorrow,' she said baldly. 'I'll be back Monday. You're on your own for the weekend, Mother.'

Deborah was lying on her bed, staring unseeingly at American football on the television.

She said, 'But you can't.'

'Yes, I can. People do it all the time.'

'You can't leave me here alone.' Deborah's voice rose in alarm.

Zoe looked at her with some sympathy. She was not so far off alarm herself, for all that Jay had said she could back out at any time. And she did not quite know what it was she was afraid of, either. But she did know that she had to face it.

'Sorry, Mother. This is something I've got to do,' she said quietly.

She was ready in the hall a good ten minutes before the limousine was due to collect her. She had packed and repacked her overnight case, to say nothing of trying on every outfit in her wardrobe. She had settled on slim navy trousers and a soft linen jacket she had shamelessly hijacked from her sister's wardrobe. She'd twirled her hair on top of her head. Inserted big hoop earrings. Dug out some gold espadrilles from the back of her wardrobe.

She looked at herself in the hall mirror. Sophisticated, she thought. Careless, even. The full casual traveller who hopped countries at less than twelve hours' notice.

Or—her sense of humour reasserted itself—she would look like that if it were not for the convulsive way she was clutching her passport. Or the way her legs trembled every time she thought of Jay.

A big black car slid smoothly to a halt outside the gate. Zoe let the curtain fall and smoothed her jacket. She felt sick.

The doorbell rang.

For a moment she almost did not answer it. The stairs were behind her. She could turn and bolt back up them.

Only—then what? Like Jay said, now she had made up her mind, the sooner she got it over with, the better. Except that it had all got a lot more complicated than she had ever imagined. Now that it included Jay, would she ever get it over with?

There was only one way to find out. Zoe's chin lifted.

'Forward into the future,' she muttered. 'Goodbye, Mother,' she called out.

There was no reply. She was not really surprised. She was mildly sorry—but she had more important things to think about just at the moment.

She opened the front door.

'I'm ready,' she said quietly. And not just to the uniformed driver.

* * *

Jay, she found, travelled business class. And he worked while he did it. He was friendly enough, but as soon as they were belted into their seats he had his papers out, making notes on the work she had given him.

'I'm going to break the back of this on the flight,' he told her. 'Then we can concentrate on showing you Venice when we get there.'

'Thank you,' said Zoe.

She was monumentally calm. So calm she even impressed herself. She certainly convinced Jay that last night's emotionalism had been dispelled. She could almost hear his sigh of relief, though he was much too civilised to say anything.

Zoe was mildly surprised at herself. This did not feel like Performance Zoe. After all, she had nothing to hide from Jay. He knew all there was to know about her. Yet nothing felt quite real.

Oh, well, no doubt it would sort itself out.

She stayed calm all through the flight, though she refused the meal and even a glass of champagne.

'Very wise,' said Jay with a faint smile.

'What?'

'Turning down the fizz. Champagne should be drunk on a terrace at sunset, to the sound of music. It loses its magic at thirty-eight thousand feet with your nose up against someone else's seat.'

Zoe laughed. 'That's because you're too tall. My nose isn't anywhere near anyone else.' She stretched, laughing, and wriggled her freshly painted toenails. 'Look at that. I've never travelled anything but economy class in my life. This is a treat all on its own.'

He did not laugh. 'Sometimes I remember how very young you are.'

She gave him a naughty look. 'Not that young. Just poor.'

Jay was ironic. 'Poverty is relative.'

She was instantly contrite. 'Of course. I should have said *relatively* poor. When my father left we still had a roof over our heads and an education in progress. The roof just crumbled a bit, that's all.'

He looked at her curiously. 'Was life difficult after he went?'

Zoe shifted her shoulders. 'We got through,' she said evasively.

He hesitated, as if he wanted to pursue the subject further. But then the screen on his laptop went dark and he was recalled to the work in hand. He went back to his draft speech.

Zoe was relieved. Perhaps he didn't know quite *all* her secrets, she thought wryly. Probably just as well if it stayed like that. After all, she was not likely to see him again once she left Culp and Christopher, was she?

After that her pleasure on the luxurious flight dimmed, for some reason. She stopped staring out into the brilliant sky and even dozed fitfully.

It was the sort of sleep where you had dreams.

She was sitting in a boat. It was a tall, silent boat, coming up fast on a fortress in the dark. She was terrified and cold and alone. She thought, *I can't do this.*

Then suddenly she wasn't in the boat any more. She was inside the fortress and running, running, running… And someone moved out of the shadows. She stopped dead, trying not to breathe. But it was hopeless. Her breathing sounded like an avalanche. A shadow detached itself from the darkness, moved towards her. She thought, *My enemy?* And then the shadow fell over her, engulfing her and—and—and—

And she woke up.

Jay took his hand off her shoulder and sat back. 'Seat belt,' he said briefly. But he gave her an odd look.

It was only a dream, Zoe told herself. Only a dream.

But she was glad that he did not try to touch her on the way from the airport to the hotel.

And when they got to the hotel she forgot fears and dreams alike in sheer amazement.

'It's a palace,' she said, awed.

Jay was signing them in. A double room. Of course. Zoe stood and stared at the cherubic trumpeters on the marvellously painted ceiling and tried to pretend that she did this all the time.

The bellboy loaded their cases onto a six-foot brass birdcage and summoned them to follow him. The elevator was discreetly hidden behind panelled doors decorated with pastel nymphs and knowing satyrs. Zoe avoided the satyrs' eyes. Jay seemed unaware.

'It probably was a palace originally,' he said indifferently. 'A merchant's palace anyway. In Venice rank strictly followed profit on the high seas. They weren't big on idle aristocrats.'

Zoe was impressed. 'I never did history,' she confessed. 'I was always more of a scientist. My degree is in chemistry.'

He gave a choke of laughter.

'What?' she said, suspecting mockery.

'And this is the woman who rebuked me for not being a people person!'

She chuckled wickedly. 'Ah, but I learn about people from life, not books.'

He shook his head. 'Well, this weekend you're going to learn about Venice if it kills me.'

And then they got to their floor and she found he had booked not just a double room but a whole suite. She was embarrassed by this extravagance, and said so disjointedly as soon as the bellboy had left, well tipped.

Jay shrugged. 'I promised you no pressure.'

It silenced her utterly.

He was disposing his things with the automatic efficiency of a man who had worked in a lot of hotel rooms. He put his laptop on a small baroque desk, plugged it in, adjusted the lighting to suit. Then he hung up his suit and a spare pair of trousers and took his sponge bag into the bathroom.

It all took about three minutes. He had finished before Zoe managed to rouse herself from her stunned stillness. She had sat down on an antique wooden chair and was staring fixedly at a lavish bowl of fruit in the middle of a rather less antique coffee table.

Jay came out of the bedroom and looked at her shrewdly.

'Get your walking shoes on,' he said briskly. 'We'll do a circuit, so you know where to find things. Shake away the aeroplane blues.'

Zoe licked her lips. 'Yes. I mean, what a good idea. Thank you.'

She gave herself several mental shakes and did as he said.

It was obvious that he knew Venice well. He took her to the Grand Canal first. But when he saw that she found the press of people almost overwhelming in the hot sunshine, he whisked her over a couple of little bridges, through a tiny square and into a herring-bone-paved side street.

To their left, the water lapped gently against stones that were green with age and watery moss. To their right, the decorated façade of a three-storeyed merchant's house cast a warm ochre shade. A cat dozed beside a marble fountain. A shutter banged back. A small boy ran out of a house and was chased back inside. And all the while the water lifted and murmured like an animal padding beside them.

'It's amazing,' said Zoe, awed.

Jay gave a long sigh of pleasure. He looked round. 'Yes. There's nowhere in the world like Venice.'

On the other side of the little canal a striped awning rolled down to shield the street from the evening sun. As if by magic, it seemed, a cake shop was appearing as the building seemed to wake out of its lazy afternoon doze. A woman came out and pushed back wooden shutters decorated with two china masks and a single elegant high-heeled shoe, to reveal a window of mouth-watering pastries. It was beautiful and strange and somehow menacing.

'How can they make a cake shop look like a carnival assignation?' said Zoe, pointing it out.

'Style. And deception. The twin principles that Venice lives by,' said Jay. He sounded pleased. 'Always has. Let me show you.'

He took her through dark little streets, across tiny canals that looked like people's private drive-ways and down main thoroughfares. The water was cool and mysterious beside their feet, like a lazy, watchful snake, Zoe thought. While the buildings were warm as toast to the touch. The colours were like every painting of Venice she had ever seen: buildings in cherry and terracotta and straw and the exact shade of crisp pastry. The landscape was studded with grey stone bridges and fountains and statues, like diamonds on a rich fabric. And through it all the sinewy, silent water.

At last they came back to the Grand Canal again. By that time Zoe's head was spinning.

'I'm lost. I thought the Grand Canal was back there.' She waved a hand behind them.

Jay looked even more pleased. 'It is. We're on the great loop of a meander. Now we cross the Accademia Bridge here, and we'll go and see the Big Attraction.'

The Piazza San Marco was full of people again. But Zoe did not care. She sank onto a rattan chair in one of the outdoor cafés and sighed with exquisite satisfaction.

'I never knew—' she said in wonder.

'You can see just as much in books, of course. Or television. But you don't sense it,' agreed Jay. He summoned a waiter with his usual ease and ordered English tea. 'Later we'll have Bellinis. I always like to leave cocktails until after dark when I'm here.'

Zoe did not quibble with that. 'You seem to know Venice very well.'

He smiled. It was one of his real smiles, not the up-and-under sexy stuff that she saw him use on clients or difficult women. It felt as if he had let his guard down and was letting her see him. More than see him. Warm her hands at the flame of his intelligence.

'Venice was the first city that reconciled me to Europe.'

'What?' She was genuinely startled.

He stretched his long legs out in front of him, screwing up his eyes. She thought he watched the tourists as if they were a mildly interesting form of wildlife.

'I'm only half-European, you know. The later flowering half. I was born in India. Kerala. That's where my mother comes from. We lived there with my grandfather until I was seven.'

Zoe was surprised. She had heard about his grandfather. 'The Brigadier?'

The passionate mouth curved. He was laughing at himself. She thought he was no longer strictly policing himself, curbing his instincts, banking down his passions. There was an alluring suggestion that he had loosed control. Oh, for the moment he was just lazily content. But potentially—Well, she could not guess. She had never seen him look like this. So relaxed. So alert. So accessible.

It made her want to touch him. More than touch. Curve against his body and stroke his skin and turn his mouth towards her and—

Careful, Zoe!

He said lazily, 'Not the Brigadier. My mother's father. He was a wholly different kettle of fish.'

She thought, He liked that grandfather a lot. Maybe even loved him. She had never thought of sexy, sophisticated Jay Christopher as loving anyone before. It was intriguing.

'What was he like?'

His face softened. 'The ideal grandfather. He knew brilliant games. He told stories. He taught me to swim—and how to recognise fish and birds and plants. He was a scholar and a philosopher. But most of all he was kind.'

Yes, he definitely loved him.

'Why did he bring you up?'

'Oh, the usual. My father was a hippy drop-out on the Maharishi trail when he met my mother. He persuaded her to leave college and go on the road with him. She got pregnant. He didn't tell his family—he said they were British snobs and he never wanted to see them again. My Indian grandfather took them both in and they married. So I was born in this wonderful house on the beach. I used to fall asleep every night to the sound of the surf. Sometimes when I close my eyes I can still hear it.'

There was a world of loss in the deep voice. Zoe leaned forward.

'When did you leave?'

'When I was seven. I told you.'

Their tea came. She drank, watching him watch the crowd.

'What happened? Did your father decide to go back to England after all?'

'No. My father was long gone by then. Later we heard he'd died of pneumonia somewhere. We were never quite sure when, exactly. But as soon as my English grandfather found out he came looking for me. They sent him my father's papers. That was how he found out that he had a grandson.' His voice changed, flattened. 'So he came and took us back to England.'

Zoe said slowly, 'And you hated it.'

Jay shrugged impatiently. 'It was okay once we got to the country. At least that was green and there were trees. London was bad. All that concrete. I was used to colours and spices and heat. Even the rains are warm in Kerala. At least on the coast, where we lived. In London everything was the colour of old chewing gum. And it smelled like wet Mackintosh.'

'Horrible!'

'To a seven-year-old, it was pretty much hell, yes.' He drank his tea, his eyes shadowed.

'But you went back?'

'My English grandfather wouldn't allow it. So, no, not until I was eighteen. And then later, of course, when I started to earn money and could afford it. But it wasn't the same.'

Zoe's heart turned over, he sounded so bleak. 'Why?'

'Me. The place was the same. Full of books and open to the sea breezes. But I'd changed.'

'Well, of course. You'd grown up.'

'It was more than that. I'd started winning races, you see. I was eighteen and I liked the buzz. And the attention.'

'Understandable.'

'Ah, but my lost grandfather told me to be careful of that. "You can like winning so much you lose sight of what it is you're doing to win," he said. But I didn't take any notice.'

She said bracingly, 'At eighteen boys don't take any notice of anyone. It's in the job description.'

His eyes lit with sudden laughter. He came out of his reverie, turning to her. 'And how do you know that?'

'My brother Harry. He tuned me out some time around fifteen.'

'Tuned *you* out? You brought him up?'

'It's been a kind of communal effort,' said Zoe ruefully. 'Mother's spaced out. Father's off pretending he's hunk of the month. We sort of brought each other up. Only I was the eldest so I did the shopping.'

Jay's eyes were warm on her. 'Then I think it's time someone spoiled you to death.'

She looked around the square and grinned from ear to ear. 'Somebody is.'

He took her hand. She thought he was going to squeeze it. Another of those brotherly caresses which she ought to be getting used to.

But he didn't. Instead he raised it to his lips. It was not a real kiss, just a brush of his lips, his breath on her knuckles. It was not sexy. It was not playful. In fact it felt oddly formal, like a declaration of some sort. It felt was as if he was honouring her in some way, like a courtier paying respect to a queen he had suddenly decided was worth it.

And it was not brotherly.

Yes! thought Zoe.

CHAPTER NINE

WHEN they had finished tea, Jay gave her a rapid and informed tour, dodging tourists.

'Venetian art was looted from everywhere in the known world,' he said, pointing at the Basilica in a friendly way. 'Carvings, columns and capitals courtesy of Genoa and Constantinople. Constantinople, of course, had already pinched a lot from China.'

And, when they got to the Doge's Palace, 'The four figures in porphyry were probably acquired after the sack of Acre. The ownership of property is provisional and strictly temporary.'

'I suppose it is,' said Zoe, entertained.

'Bridge of Sighs,' he said waving his hand at the dark little prison tunnel over the small canal. 'Once you crossed that, you stopped caring about property, I guess.'

She shivered. 'It's not all joy, is it, Venice?'

'What is? It has *energy*.' He paused. 'And that gives me an idea. I think I know how to close my speech, now. Zoe, you're a genius.'

And he rushed her back to the hotel at top speed.

In the suite he flung himself at the laptop computer immediately. Zoe wandered around a while, self-conscious again. But he was so absorbed in what he was doing that it was impossible to remain embarrassed.

She decided to bath and wash the dust out her hair.

'Fine,' said Jay absently, his fingers flying, his eyes on the screen.

So much for the evil seducer, pouncing on her the moment she got her clothes off, thought Zoe with irony. Not very flattering. But somehow—right.

She sang in the bath.

When she padded out, wrapped in the hotel's fluffy white robe with her hair in a towel, Jay was standing in the long open windows looking out at the street below. She went to stand beside him.

'Look at that,' he said softly.

The building opposite was arched and columned fantastically. The roofline had a carved frieze that looked as if it had been done with curling tongs. It was built of biscuit-coloured stone, with heavily carved wooden doors of treacle-brown. Zoe knew the colours because she had seen them earlier. But the sunset turned them to pure gold.

'Oh,' she said on long breath of wonder.

He put his arm round her and they stood looking—at the golden evening, the busy pavement, the gondoliers in their long dark gondolas. And the water, darker than anything else, unimaginably dark below the surface of brazen ripples that were conferred by the dying sun.

'See,' he said. 'Energy. Mystery. Everything. God, I love this place.'

'I can see.'

He jumped then, and looked down at her.

'Feeling okay?' he asked, his eyes searching.

Zoe knew he was not talking about her health, or the effects of sightseeing, or even the seductively lazy bath. He was checking to see that she did not want to back out yet. She felt totally cared for.

'Feeling wonderful,' she told him honestly.

Jay gave her the widest grin she had ever seen.

'Great,' he said with enthusiasm. 'Then here we go for Venice by night.'

She wore soft silky trousers and a gold strappy top that looked a lot more expensive than it was. She gave up on her hair, which just turned into a waterfall of fox-brown curls as a result.

'No jewellery?' said Jay, emerging from the bedroom in one of his spectacular silk shirts.

'Forgot it—sorry. I don't have much, and wear less. Does it matter?'

'On the contrary,' he said with a maddeningly mysterious smile.

She decided not to challenge him. Tonight the shirt was peacock-green. It made him look like an emperor. You challenged emperors at your peril.

She told him so, and he laughed.

'Tonight we're on the same side,' he said. 'No challenge necessary.' They strolled through the streets hand in hand. Like friends. Like lovers.

The gold of the miraculous sunset slowly died away, as if someone had pulled a cloth of gold out towards the sea. That left the lights that were set by people. Windows and streetlamps and little lanterns on the prows of the gondolas.

'They look slightly dangerous,' said Zoe, as a gondola swept up to some steps and some laughing passengers climbed out.

He was surprised. 'Do you think so? They're perfectly safe. The gondoliers are incredibly expert. It runs in the family, you know.'

'Not dangerous like that. I suppose I mean sinister. As if they're full of clever men plotting.'

He hugged her, laughing.

'I shall have to bring you here during carnival. The masks can be very beautiful, but they are unsettling.'

Zoe loved him hugging her. She rubbed her cheek against the peacock silk shoulder. She felt proud and mischievous at the same time.

His arm tightened. 'Venice has made sinister an art form. You know they used to have a Signori di Notte? It was specially set up to keep the peace at night.' His voice dropped thrillingly. 'The time of assassins, thieves and spies.'

Zoe wrinkled her nose at the assassins. 'And lovers,' she pointed out.

His arm was suddenly a steel bar.

'And lovers,' he agreed in a still voice.

That was when the trembling started. A slow, sweet, deep trembling that she had never felt before.

And suddenly she thought—Could he be right? Could it be that she had never wanted to make love to anyone because she had never been in love? It was not the fashionable answer. Not even the rational one, in some way. And yet she felt in her bones that no one before had been possible. And Jay was more than possible. He was the only one.

Nonsense, she told herself. It was the night and Venice and all the hocus pocus of gondolas and streets that weren't streets, but treacherous, shifting, mysterious water. This was fantasy, pure and simple.

But his arm round her wasn't fantasy. Nor was the account of his childhood. She was sure that nobody else in Culp and Christopher knew about that.

And nor was the look in his eyes.

She had seen Jay's up-and-under, sex-is-a-state-of-mind look. She had had the benefit of the sexy stare straight into her eyes. She had seen him challenging and she had seen him shameless. In all the weeks she had known him she had never seen him look at anyone like this.

Steady. Slightly questioning. Sure, and yet—not sure.

She thought—*I'm the one to make him sure. The next move is mine.*

She waited for the alarm to hit her. After all, only last night in her mother's room she had been all but falling apart with panic. It did not come. It felt right that the next move was hers. And when the time was right she would make it.

Jay took her to a candlelit restaurant. The tables were covered in heavy damask and an array of crystal, and the conversation was the low hum of people who took their food seriously. He was obviously known there, too.

The waiter led them to a secluded table, murmuring confidentially.

Jay nodded. 'Two Bellinis to start with, Carlo.'

Jay held the deeply red cushioned chair for her. The table was by a floor-to-ceiling window, open to the shifting murmurous night.

'Fit for lovers?' he murmured in her ear.

Zoe bit back a naughty smile.

'Very appropriate,' she assured him gravely.

His eyes were warm hazel and very close as he smiled down at her. It was like a kiss.

'I'm relieved.'

He sat in his own seat and took her hand proprietorially. Just as if that was what he always did.

Zoe's heart fluttered. She was not alarmed—but this was new. And new took dealing with.

Still, she could deal with it. She could deal with anything. She swallowed and summoned up all her hot babe repartee.

'Do you do a lot of this sort of thing?' she asked chattily.

Jay's smile did not change. 'No. You're my first,' he told her.

And watched with pleasure as she choked.

Two drinks arrived. They were the colour of sunrise and they hissed.

'Our Bellinis,' said Jay. 'Local invention. Champagne and peach juice. And probably a secret ingredient, though no Venetian barman will tell.'

He toasted her silently. They clinked glasses and drank.

Zoe considered. 'A bit sweet. Touch of the alcopop.'

It was Jay's turn to choke. 'Don't tell them that,' he begged. 'It would be like insulting the flag.'

Zoe twinkled at him. 'Oh, all right then. You're no fun, though.'

'Just trying to watch out for you,' he said peacefully. 'But if you think it would be exciting to get us thrown out, go right ahead.'

She laughed aloud. 'No, no. You're the expert. I'll do what you tell me.'

He took her hand to his lips again. 'That's quite a responsibility. I'll try not to let you down.'

The inner trembling increased. It shook through her. Like an earthquake getting ready to break. Like a drowsing lion flexing its muscles.

Jay looked at her all the time.

Zoe did not notice what they ate. She knew the waiter and Jay discussed the food briefly and the wine at length. She remembered fish so fresh that it tasted of the sea, wine that slid over her palate like distilled flowers. But then even the water tasted as if it had just bubbled up from some fresh spring.

What's happening to me? Getting carried away by the taste of water, for heaven's sake?

But it wasn't the water. It wasn't even the marvellous wine. Or the luxury. Or the glamour that was Venice. Or the starry night. Not even the warm wind on her bare arms as they left, though it made her shiver voluptuously.

'Cold? Or do you want to walk?' asked Jay softly.

Zoe swallowed hard. The time was right.

'I'm not cold,' she said deliberately. 'And I don't want to walk.'

He went very still. 'Home, then,' he said.

And summoned a gondola.

In the suite Zoe thought he would lead her straight through to the bedroom. He did not. Instead he switched on a couple of the table-lamps and drew her towards the couch. She sat obediently, but nerves made her clumsy. A couple of the luxuriously fat cushions plumped onto the floor.

Jay sat down beside her and took her hands.

'You're shaking,' he said gently. 'Don't shake, my love.'

'I-I don't seem to be able to stop,' Zoe said candidly. She tried to lock her jaw. It did not work. 'S-silly, isn't it?'

'No,' he said in a caressing voice. He pushed her hair gently off her face. 'No, it's not silly at all. It's just unnecessary. We won't do anything you don't want. I promise.'

'Th-thank you,' she said politely.

He gave a shaken little laugh. 'And you don't believe a word of it.'

Zoe gulped. 'Yes, I do.'

He turned her to face him. 'Really?'

She moistened her lips and saw his eyes darken.

'R-really,' she said uncertainly.

Did they darken because of her? Was it possible? A super-sophisticate like Jay Christopher?

Yet he did not feel like a super-sophisticate, sitting here beside her. So close. So reassuringly strong. So alarmingly hot. He felt like—the only man in the world she wanted to make love to her.

She suddenly realised why she had ducked out of the arms of all the Johns and Alastairs and Simons. She had liked them. She had enjoyed their company. At least twice she had desperately wanted it to work. But, in the still, quiet core of her, she had known she did not—quite—trust them. It had just not been *right.* And now it was.

She trusted Jay. Totally.

She tried to tell him and could not find the words. So she reached for him instead.

Jay took her in his arms with care. The memory of that earlier kiss was not a good one. It did not exactly haunt him. But he could not forget how she had looked as she scrubbed his touch off her mouth.

In spite of that she had trusted him with her secret, though. Now she was trusting him to make the experience a good one.

That was a tough one. All through dinner she had sat beside him trembling. She thought he did not know. But he was too alert to her every move not to feel it.

Hell, be honest, Jay. You want her so much you can hardly see straight. Every time she breathes in your blood surges. Of course you knew she was trembling. You even wanted her to tremble harder—only because of what you were doing to her, not because of her own apprehension.

Well, forget what he wanted. He had a task to do here. And that was to get her so fogged up with lust and curiosity that she forgot how terrified she was. Who knew better than he how to do just that?

He began to kiss her gently, teasingly. First her hand—yes, he had seen the way she reacted to that. Her bare shoulders. Her throat. The scent of her skin made his head swim.

But he clamped down hard on his own reactions. This was for her, he told himself. This was for *her*.

He slid the thin strap down her bare, warm arm. He remembered how the bra strap had slipped under the sheer provocation of that black chiffon shirt the first time he saw her. His body quickened at the too explicit memory. In spite of himself, his hands grew urgent.

Zoe gave a small moan. At once he loosened his hold.

But she turned on him, her own hands suddenly demanding, and kissed him fiercely.

Jay shut his eyes. Careful, he told himself. Careful!

But he did not tell Zoe. More cushions hit the floor as she writhed against him.

'Please,' she said in a panting under-voice. 'Please.'

She jumped up, kicking her espadrilles away, and, taking him by the hand, half ran to the bedroom.

Jay knew it was going too fast. He tried to slow her down. But it seemed as if she was caught up in some feverish drive of her own and couldn't hear him. She let him take her clothes off but not as slowly as he wanted. And she tore off his own.

'Zoe—'

But she pulled him down onto the bed with her, her soft hair all tangled and her eyes as wide as a fox in a trap. He could not bear to think of his Zoe trapped.

'Stop this,' Jay said with authority.

She froze.

He unclenched her frantic fingers from his neck.

'This,' he said, 'should be a lot more fun. Now, will you stop trying to do the driving and trust me?'

She bit her lip. But he saw the fierce, trapped look die out of her eyes and breathed a private sigh of relief.

'Better,' he said. 'Now, concentrate. Make notes, if you like. We need to find out what you like.'

He was thorough. He had plenty of experience to build on. But he was hungrier to satisfy her than he had been for anything since his very first race. Since the last time he hadn't been sure he could win, Jay acknowledged wryly.

'This?' he said, working his way up from her toes. 'This? How about this?'

He was rewarded. At first she was surprised. Polite, but surprised. Then intrigued. Then—he knew exactly when, because her breathing changed and her limbs seemed to unfold somehow as her muscles relaxed instinctively—the first unselfconscious quiver of response ran through her.

It was going to be all right, thought Jay. He should have been exultant. But suddenly all he felt was a chill. Almost grief.

He could not understand it. It was going to be all right, after all. Zoe was going to come with him on this. Venice, the night, the wine—they had all done their stuff. Good old Venice. He tried to be grateful.

But there was a little pain round his heart, like a rose splinter that he had picked up a long, long time ago and not noticed until now.

Venice had got Zoe so far. And now it was up to him to get her the rest of the way. It was what he was good at, after all. He had walked away from so many women into his healing solitude. And, however sad they had been, however lonely, they had never said that he was not an attentive lover.

Remember that, Jay. That's why you're qualified to do this thing for her.

He kissed the soft flesh just inside her elbow. Then, overwhelmed, buried his face against her for a moment.

'You smell so good,' he said, shaken.

He lifted his head and she met his eyes for a long, long moment. Her own widened. The room was full of silence and shadows. For a moment it felt impossible to tell where he left off and she began.

Zoe said his name on a wondering note.

Jay's heart seemed to contract in his breast.

Don't get carried away. There's only one thing you can do for this woman. So make damn sure you do it right.

He used all his skill to arouse her. His blood pounded but he stayed slow, deliberate. He knew exactly how to inflame her senses, one by one, with exquisite precision. And he did it. Her anxieties, her self consciousness, did not stand a chance. *She* did not stand a chance. This was Jay Christopher, bent on the seduction of his life.

He felt her every response, the little tiny ripples and the big, building need that swept all inhibitions out of its path. It seemed as if her senses uncurled at his touch, like a flower turning towards sunlight. It moved Jay more than he would have believed possible. He kissed her lingeringly.

Zoe clung. He knew from the way she writhed in his arms that she could not wait much longer.

Then he let her do what she wanted.

She urged him inside her. He hesitated only a moment. But he was not superhuman and she was breathless with an imperative need that he recognised even if she didn't.

It was a mistake. A terrible mistake. He knew it at once and froze, shocked.

Zoe cried out. 'No. Leave me alone. I can't bear it.'

He nearly did. But then he thought how much it had cost her to get here. How much she had trusted him to get her through this.

An inner voice jeered. *You're supposed to be the expert, Jay. Can't you do it after all?*

He paused, agonised. Hardly believing what he was doing, he held himself very still. But he did not withdraw.

He said with difficulty, 'Zoe, my love, we need to get this over.'

Jay realised too late that he had called her 'my love'. What was he thinking of? Love was never part of their bargain. He could have bitten his tongue out. But it was impossible to recall it.

He did not notice that he said 'we'. But Zoe did. She stopped thinking about her straining flesh and stared up at him, amazed.

Zoe, my love! She could not believe it. She had asked him for practical help. Was she being given the moon without asking? Without even suspecting it was available?

She touched her palm to his warm shoulder in wonder. He felt as if he were on fire.

He still did not move. But he said urgently, 'Darling, if you make me stop now, we've got it all to do again.'

We! Again! She swallowed shakily.

He was supporting himself on his elbows, but he touched his fingers to her face. It was as fleeting as the thistledown that blew past her cheek in the summer garden at home. Gone before she had time to turn her head into the caress. Zoe felt cheated.

But Jay was saying soberly, 'I know I can't stop it hurting. But I can get you through it quickly.' He smiled down at her, straight into her eyes. 'It's what I promised, after all.'

She nearly did not recognise him, his eyes were so blazing with tenderness.

'Think,' he said softly. 'Just once and you don't have to dread it ever again.'

That smile made her head spin. It also made her feel brave. She thought, *Smile at me like that and I don't have to dread anything.*

She nearly said so. But she was shy. Crazily shy, in the circumstances. And not sure that it was what he wanted to hear. And suddenly bodies seemed the best communicators after all.

She ran her palms over his shoulders, savouring the warmth and strength and sheer otherness of him.

'Oh, well,' she said, doing her best to keep it light. 'In for a penny, in for a pound, I suppose. Go—' She broke off, gasping.

He had delivered one clean, swift thrust and pain tore through her like a typhoon.

From a long way away, she heard him say, 'Oh, *love*.'

Eventually the nuclear cloud blew away and she opened her eyes. She was lying on the big gilded bed in a room full of antiques and the man who made her head spin was lying propped on one golden arm, watching her.

'Zoe?'

'Present,' she said, trying to make a joke of it. Her voice cracked.

His mouth tightened. 'That was unforgivable. I should never have—'

But she stopped him by putting her fingers over his mouth. It was amazing how good it felt to have the right to do that, to touch his lips.

'Don't. It's over. Like you said.' Her voice got stronger. 'About time, too.'

His jaw was so tight it must hurt. 'I'm sorry. You were unlucky,' he said curtly.

Zoe brushed her lips against his naked shoulder quickly. She was not quite so sure she had the right to do that, and didn't want to risk rejection.

'*We* were unlucky,' she corrected.

She fell back among the pillows, eyes closed. She was not shy, she told herself rebelliously. It would be ridiculous to be shy after making love to the man. Well, sort of making love to him. And she was a twenty-first century independent woman, after all. She just did not feel up to meeting his eyes quite yet, that was all.

He brushed the hair off her face softly. 'You're a kind girl.' He sounded very far away.

Suddenly she wanted to say *I love you*. But she was absolutely sure that she did not have the right to do that. Well, she thought, brave behind her closed eyelids, not yet.

And suddenly she thought— He booked a suite. He may not even want to spend the night in my bed. They say he never stays the night, don't they? Her eyes flew open in horror and she sat up.

'What is it?' said Jay, concerned. 'Are you hurt? Do you want something? Water?'

'No—but the couch—the sitting room.' She was incoherent in her alarm at encroaching on him.

Jay's face was rigid. He did not touch her.

But he said quietly, 'No. Sleep with me.'

She searched his face. Were they wrong about his rule against spending the night with his lover? Or was tonight something that broke his rules?

She thought of that blaze of tenderness she had surprised on his face. That had not looked like a man who was keeping his own rules of detachment, either. And he had called her *Zoe, my love*.

The first time she saw him—the very first time, in his sunset silk shirt—she had thought, This is love at first sight! And laughed at herself. Well, she was way beyond laughter now. She shook her head, dazed.

He misinterpreted the gesture.

He said almost inaudibly, 'Sleep in my arms. Let me do that for you, at least. For both of us.'

And suddenly Zoe saw how hurt he was. How angry with himself. For a moment her body had felt as if it was splitting apart, but it was not Jay's fault. He had used all his skill and all his knowledge and it had not been enough. He was raw with self-disgust and she had brought him to it. It was up to her to put it right.

She said, 'Hold me, Jay.'

His arms closed round her. He carried their locked bodies back among the pillows very carefully.

Her eyes closed tight at once. But she was not asleep, he knew. He did not challenge her. And eventually her breathing slowed, became regular, and he knew she had fallen asleep at last.

But Jay lay there, with her sleeping head against his shoulder, and stared open-eyed into the darkness.

CHAPTER TEN

ZOE woke to the sound of bells. She stretched languorously, not opening her eyes. *I feel different,* she thought drowsily.

Different and peaceful and somehow proud. And surprised. As if she had won a war that she had been fighting for too long.

I thought I was going to get deeper and deeper into lies for the rest of my life. And now it's all behind me.

But much, much more important—what was in front of her? The future suddenly looked a lot less predictable. It was exciting.

I slept in the arms of Jay Christopher, who never spends the night. And who called me his love. This is a very surprising day.

Zoe gave a long, long sigh of pure satisfaction. The bells pealed out joyously, celebrating life and victory and morning. A wide schoolgirl grin started behind her eyelids.

'Too right,' she told the bells, eyes still closed, savouring the triumph that was her life.

She opened her eyes and sat up, stretching her arms exuberantly above her head.

'Today is the first day of the rest of my life. Look out world!'

And it was so easy.

Thanks to Jay. She would never have screwed her courage to the sticking point if he hadn't held her to it. She owed him, big time. She had to tell him. She turned—

That was when she realised that she was alone in the bed.

For a moment she was taken aback. The words had been on the tip of her tongue, all ready to bubble out. But his pillow looked as if it had been pounded to pieces during the night and there was no sign of Jay at all.

'Oh,' said Zoe, her mood temporarily flattened.

But then she thought, He's probably an early riser. Maybe he's gone out jogging. Or he couldn't sleep through the bells.

The schoolgirl grin broke out again.

She got up, pulling the hotel's bathrobe over her nakedness, and padded out to the sitting room.

The floor-to-ceiling windows were flung wide to the brilliant morning. And Jay was standing at one of them, looking out over the canal. No shirt, but he was wearing dark trousers. His hair was rumpled and his feet were bare. Zoe's heart lurched.

I slept in that man's arms last night. I want him.

He had his hands in his pockets and he was frowning. Lost in his thoughts, he certainly did not hear her.

She padded across to him and slipped both hands round his arm. He jumped, stiffening. Zoe was too happy to worry about it.

'Listen to them,' she said, rubbing her face companionably against his shoulder. 'Triumph in a few notes.'

He did not return the caress. But, after the tiniest pause, he said in an amused voice, 'The bells? They're supposed to be calling the faithful to prayer, you know.'

'Nah. It's Venice showing off. I'm the best, you suckers.'

She waved her arms above her head, taunting the rest of the world.

Released, he moved away from her. 'You're very chirpy.'

Zoe was in tearing spirits and saw no reason to hide it. 'I'm wonderful.'

Some of the constraint fell away from him. 'Glad to hear it. Do you want coffee?'

She stretched again, beaming. Below, the gilded water gleamed. Sunbeams struck diamond rainbows off the columns and colonnades of the square palace opposite. The morning air felt sharp and warm at the same time.

'I want everything,' she said with relish.

He laughed.

'I want to do everything. I want to see everything. I want to *fly*.' She flung her arms wide, embracing Venice, life and the universe.

'Start with coffee,' Jay advised.

She realised that there was a tray on the coffee table. He poured her a cup and brought it over to her.

'Not as hot as it was, sorry.'

She took it, her exuberance dimming a little. 'Have you been up long?'

'A while,' he said uncommunicatively.

She remembered—*he doesn't stay the night*. It was only a tiny pinprick in the fabric of her delight, but it was there all the same.

She said ruefully, 'Ouch. My fault, I suppose? Did I snore?'

Jay looked startled. Then he shook his head, smiling. 'No. You were very well behaved.' He raised his coffee cup to her. 'A positive pleasure to sleep with.'

Zoe twinkled back at him. 'That's a relief.'

He looked at her searchingly. 'You really are all right this morning?'

The grin broke out again. She could not stop it.

'I'm bloody marvellous.'

'You're not just—saying that?'

'Oh, come on. Would I?'

'Yes,' he said unexpectedly.

Zoe stared. 'What? Why?'

His eyes were greeny-hazel and oddly remote. 'Because you're kind and you're brave and you tell people what they want to hear,' he answered literally. 'I want to hear that I didn't hurt you last night. So, hey presto, my wish is granted. This morning, for one day only, the Zoe Brown all-singing, all-dancing extravaganza.'

She pulled the robe tighter round her. Suddenly the crisp morning seemed chilly.

'You're crazy.'

'No, I'm not,' said Jay intensely. 'I'm a man with a bad conscience trying to get the truth out of a world-class actress.'

Zoe winced. But she said with spirit, 'And to think you had the gall to call *me* neurotic! I think you can't have had enough sleep. I must have snored after all, and you're just lying about it to be kind.'

Their eyes met in a duel that she did not wholly understand.

She dropped the sarcasm. 'Look at me, Jay,' she said quietly. 'If I were any more pleased with myself I'd burst.'

There was a pause. For a moment his eyes flickered, as if he were confused. Then he shrugged and turned away. 'That's all right, then.'

They talked about Venice. And the day's itinerary. And breakfast. And her crazy family. She even made a joke about Deborah's midnight pot roast. They laughed and they were friends.

But it dimmed the day a bit.

Zoe had an energising shower, then climbed into slim pale trousers and a crop top. Her mirrored image looked back at her, wide eyed and—excited.

Excited?

'The start of the rest of my life,' she murmured. 'And his.'

She went back into the bedroom, brushing her curls vigorously. Jay was standing by the bed. He turned—and for a moment she hardly recognised him. His face was a rigid mask but his eyes looked agonised.

'What is it?' she said involuntarily, going to him.

'So little blood for so much pain.'

She realised he had been looking at the stained sheet. Her heart turned over. She took his hand. It felt inert in hers. As if he did not want her to touch him. Zoe began to feel alarmed.

'That's nothing,' she said. 'There'd be more blood from a grazed knee.'

'I hurt you.'

Zoe's voice rose. 'Okay, so I made a fuss. But this is *nothing*. The burn hurt more than that.'

Jay detached himself. 'But *I* didn't burn you.'

And the day dimmed a little more.

They both made an effort, though. Zoe resumed brushing her hair. Jay shook off his constraint, raised an eyebrow at the way her curls clung to the brush and said, 'I've never seen hair sizzle before.'

'Curls,' said Zoe, refusing to acknowledge the constraint between them. 'The bane of my life. No serious person has curls. I'll probably have to shave my head before I can embark on a serious career.'

'Don't you dare,' said Jay.

She hoped he would touch her hair then. He didn't. But at least he watched with apparent fascination as she twined it into a pony tail and clipped it round with a bright turquoise elasticated fastening with a daisy button it.

'You look about twelve,' he commented.

Zoe narrowed her eyes at him. 'I've got a degree in chemistry and on-the-job experience of all necessary life skills from plumbing to party-giving. I am not twelve.'

The constraint eased a bit more.

'Sorry,' said Jay, amused.

He opened the door of the suite for her.

'Okay, I happen to have been a little slow in launching my great career,' Zoe allowed. 'I have been taking stock of my available options.'

'I'm sure there are hundreds,' he said politely.

And a whole new dimension of them since last night. She bit back a grin. 'Just watch me.'

He touched her hair then, ruffling it as if she were the twelve-year-old he'd mentioned. 'You're a tonic, Discovery.'

They went down in the cherub-festooned elevator.

Breakfast was served with maximum pomp in the restaurant.

'You can't possibly need that many plates and glasses to eat a croissant,' said Zoe, torn between amazement and contempt.

'This is an international hotel,' Jay told her, entertained. 'You can have everything from hominy grits to ham and cheese. To say nothing of that pickled fish that the Scandinavians eat. You need a variety of fighting irons to deal with a menu like that.'

'There is no way I'm eating pickled fish for breakfast,' announced Zoe, horrified.

'Relax. It's not obligatory.'

And nor was the restaurant, apparently. He led her through it to an open air terrace. The tables there had bright gingham cloths instead of stiff white damask, and a marked diminution in the crockery and glassware.

'You get your own orange juice and buns from that table under the awning,' Jay told her. 'They come and take orders for whatever else you want. Coffee, tea, eggs, mixed grill.'

She wrinkled her nose at him. 'And I suppose you come here regularly, too. What on earth do you do for kicks? You've done everything in the world before,' she complained.

At once he went very still. 'Not everything.'

At once Zoe recalled his stillness this morning, when she'd found him frowning out at the canal. And later, contemplating her physical hurt.

She could have kicked herself. *Damn! Why can't I learn to keep my mouth shut? Now he's thinking about last night again.*

He obviously *hated* everything about last night. The day dimmed a lot more.

But then she squared her shoulders. Oh, well, there was nothing she could do about it. Except get back to neutral subjects as fast as she could—and try to avoid putting her foot in it again.

She said lightly, 'Well, enough to give me some considered vocational advice. What do you think I should do as a career?'

He relaxed visibly. 'What do you want to do?'

'If I knew that, I'd be doing it.'

'Okay, let's look at it another way. What did you like about university?'

'Friends. The course. Independence,' said Zoe promptly.

The waiter arrived and they ordered.

When he left, Jay said, 'Your course. What did you like about that?'

She chuckled. 'Oh, chemistry is wonderful. So elegant. Everything fits, if you know what I mean. The boys used to like it because they were licensed to blow things up. But I just loved the ideas. I used to draw patterns of chemical structures. And I'd work on an experiment for weeks if I had to, until I got it right.'

He smiled, ticking off on his fingers. 'Okay. No violence. Plenty of order. Plus patience. And persistence. Sounds good.'

She pulled a face. 'Not very marketable. I mean, I'd have quite liked to go into food chemistry, but you need a second degree and I wasn't good enough for that.'

'Don't put yourself down,' he said. 'There is a very strong movement to offer you a full-time job at Culp and Christopher.'

Zoe was genuinely astonished. 'You're joking.'

His mouth tilted with wry self-mockery. 'On the contrary. I'm fighting it off with all my might.'

'Oh.' She did not like that. But her curiosity was too great for her. 'Why?'

His look was ironic. 'You're seriously asking me why I don't want you working for me?'

She winced. 'No,' she said hastily, 'I think I'll pass on that. Tell me why the fans—my few fans,' she added acidly, 'want to take me on in the first place. What have I got that would be any use to you—er—Culp and Christopher?'

He hesitated.

'See?' She tried not to let her disappointment show. She did it well. So Performance Zoe was not quite dead yet, then. 'Nothing. It would be just another job making the tea and running around after everyone else.'

'It wouldn't.'

She was disbelieving. 'Really? So—hypothetically—what can you seriously see me doing at Culp and Christopher?'

Jay's eyes danced. 'Actually, you're not going to like this.'

Zoe's eyes narrowed. 'I don't like making the tea, but it doesn't kill me. Come on. Tell the truth and shame the devil.'

'Well, I—that is they—the others—Tom and his cohorts—want you because you're ordinary.'

He was right. She did not like it. She narrowed her eyes at him in a glare.

'See? I told you you wouldn't like it.'

'Ordinary—how?'

'Well, we've got a bunch of specialists at the moment.' Jay gave her that sudden blazing smile that kept even the most cynical employee on his side when times got rough.

She mistrusted it deeply, even under normal circumstances. Here, this morning, she thought, *He's hiding something.*

He went on, 'Actually, they're all oddballs. Though we don't say it, of course. Molly is nearly as weird as the rockers she hangs with. Or she was until she found herself a regular guy. And the Fab Ab, of course. Our token upper class bird and Interpreter to the Seriously Rich. Lady Abigail, no less. Does good work, too, in spite of the handle. Then there's Sam—she knows movies, and quotes the screenplay of everything Harrison Ford's ever done. But there isn't one regular soap-watching, romance-reading, family-running woman in the whole bunch.'

Zoe sat very still. *What is he hiding?*

The smile intensified until she thought she would burn up in it.

'I don't call you Discovery for nothing. That's why.'

Zoe nodded slowly. *What doesn't he want me to see?*

She said aloud, 'I'm not ordinary. I woke to bells, the sun is shining and I'm in love.'

His blazing smile flickered, seemed to freeze for moment.

She gave a soft laugh. A soft, false laugh. Oh, Performance Zoe was back with a vengeance. So much for hello to the rest of her life!

'Relax, Jay. With Venice, I was going to say. I've fallen in love with Venice.'

'Of course you have,' he agreed.

Their coffee arrived, and with it eggs and a great bowl of fresh fruit.

Zoe picked up her knife and fork and attacked her scrambled eggs with gusto.

'Gotta keep my strength up. Gotta lotta sights to see.'

It was a lifeline, the sightseeing. As soon as they finished breakfast Jay bought her a guide-book and they retraced the steps of yesterday's walk. Only this time they went inside the palaces, the museums, the galleries. Jay offered to buy her an instant camera but she refused.

'I want to drink it in. Hold it in my memory. I can't do that if I'm peering through a little hole taking pictures all the time,' she said crisply. Adding conscientiously, 'But thank you.'

He nodded. 'You're a real original, aren't you?'

She sent him a swift look. 'Not so ordinary, after all?'

Jay sighed. 'I knew I should never have told you that.'

She had got her exuberance back. Okay, some of it was performance. But some of it was the sheer energy of last night.

Zoe danced along beside a weathered stone wall. 'I forgive you.'

'Thank you,' he said gravely.

She knew she was being teased. She turned round and skipped backwards in front of him, looking wicked.

'Who wants to be a rotten old spin doctor anyway?'

The thin handsome face lit with laughter. 'Oh, quite. You sound like my Indian grandfather.'

She raised her eyebrows. 'Sounds like a good guy.'

'Yes.' His face softened wonderfully when he talked about his Indian grandfather, she saw. 'That's more or less what he said the last time I saw him.' His eyes were very green. He looked away. 'He did not like what I'd become. He'd like it even less now.'

Zoe stopped dead. Big stuff coming, she thought.

She said carefully, 'Do you? Dislike what you've become, I mean?'

He hesitated. 'Maybe.'

She sucked her teeth. After a pause, she said, 'Know why?'

He came back from whatever dark place he had been visiting. 'I do, and it's all too easy for me.' He hesitated, as if he was struggling for words. 'When I was running I had to train every day, in a structured way. No quick fixes. No spin, if you like. I was as good as I deserved to be. Oh, sometimes I got a little lucky. But I couldn't *talk* my performance up. If it was sub-standard, it was sub-standard. I couldn't argue with the results.'

She digested this. 'Yes—but life is not as simple as a race, is it?

Jay looked at her, arrested. 'What do you mean?'

'Well, when you do one of your public relations campaigns you're telling people about values. Not just about who won. About how you measure the winning.' She stopped. 'I don't now what I'm talking about. Sorry.'

Jay said slowly, 'For a woman who is suspicious of spin doctoring you are making a lot of sense.'

But Zoe was embarrassed. She started walking again, energetically, to hide the fact. 'How did you get into PR anyway?'

Jay's face lit with spontaneous amusement. 'Self-defence.'

Zoe goggled. 'What?'

'It was after I won my first big medal. A couple of journalists made a complete prat of me. Entirely my own fault. So I thought—I'll look into this. Next time I won I got the story I wanted into the press—and athletics got the boost it should have done first time around. So then I thought—there's a job here. I've been passing on what I learned then ever since.'

'I see,' said Zoe slowly. She thought about the research she had done for his speech tomorrow. 'But it's more than that, isn't it? I mean, it's about more than celebrities planting stories?'

'Yes.'

'So tell me about that.'

But he flung up a hand. 'It's my day off. You want to hear the Jay Christopher Philosophy of Public Relations, you listen to my speech tomorrow.'

She was surprised. She had not been at all sure that he was going to let her go to the conference. She'd half expected him to hide the fact that she was with him. It broke all his professional rules, after all.

'You want me to come? Really?'

'Couldn't do it without you,' he said lightly.

She didn't believe him. But it warmed her almost as much as if she did.

Instead she tossed her head so that her pony tail swung and said carelessly, 'Then you got it.' She thought about it. 'I'll even give you my totally ordinary thoughts on your analysis,' she added wickedly.

Jay stayed calm under this provocation. 'I look forward to it.'

Zoe looked at him with deep suspicion. 'Do you? Why?'

'The right-hand-side bias,' he said mysteriously.

'What?'

Jay was bland. 'Tom Skellern's profile analysis.'

Zoe frowned. 'You mean that pointless test? What about it?'

Jay stopped and leaned on the wall, looking down into the busy canal. Dark gondolas jostled each other in duels for precedence. They just managed not to touch as the winner swept away with a flourish. Vaporetti chugged. People on the other bank strolled hand in hand. He propped his elbows on the river wall and locked his hands together.

He said, 'If you're interested in the PR business there's a spectrum of response. Male attitudes at the extreme left, female at the right. Most people are somewhere in the middle. But you particularly are hard on the right-hand side. Very girly.'

'Girly?' Zoe was revolted and did not try to hide it.

He smiled. 'Tom's score calls the category that you come into the Boyfriend's Dream.'

She tensed. 'Oh?'

'Sorry about that,' he said, unconvincingly. 'Touch of political incorrectness there. But the message is—you're all woman. And,' he added with an abrupt return to the prosaic, 'there won't be a lot of them at the conference tomorrow.'

'Then I'll be glad to fill in,' said Zoe between her teeth.

All woman!

If only he meant it. And if only it was what Jay really thought, rather than the result of Tom Skellern's multiple choice questionnaire, she thought, depressed. If only it was what he thought after last night, in her arms!

She turned and leaned on the wall beside him, turning her head away. She had done her best to stay bright all day. But now she could not deny the emptiness between them any more.

Oh, he had made love to her, fair enough. He had said he would and he had kept his promise. More than kept his promise, she thought. There was warmth round her heart when she thought of the care he had taken of her.

But today, though he was trying, he was as far away as the moon. Zoe kept trying to work out why and she simply could not find the answer. He was not embarrassed, of course. He was much too sophisticated for that. And not emotionally involved, either. That had been implicit in the deal.

So what was it? Something was wrong; she knew it.

And then she remembered him saying, a lifetime ago, *'Once you've made up your mind to do something you don't want to, the best thing is to get it over with.'*

Well, it felt like a lifetime ago. But it had only been Friday night. Less than two days. And he had got it over, all right, hadn't he? At the time she had thought he was talking about her feelings. But now she realised he had been talking about his own.

He hadn't wanted to do it. But he had.

And, in doing so, he had caused her a little pain. He had not been prepared for that. Zoe had seen how it had shocked him.

Hell, she thought, staring out across afternoon Venice. I've made him ashamed of himself. He's never going to forgive me.

CHAPTER ELEVEN

THE rest of that day they walked, until Venice was swimming before Zoe's eyes.

Then Jay took her to some famous bar for a drink; then another, less famous, for jazz. They ate in a bistro. It was full and noisy, with families and a huge party of people who turned out to be gondoliers at the central table. Jay chatted to them in easy Italian and he and Zoe joined them in toasting the newest member of the group, for whom the dinner was being held.

When they left she nearly said, We're going to have to talk. We have to share a bed tonight and we have been walking round the subject all day.

But Jay got in first.

'They told me where the best club is,' he said. 'They're not as ageist in Venice as they are in London. They'll probably even let me in.'

They did. It was not so different from the clubs where Zoe danced at home. Maybe a bit smaller, and the drinks were different. More wine, less vodka. But the atmosphere was the same and so was the music.

She abandoned herself to the familiar intoxication of the music. There was nothing else to do. Jay was evidently quite determined not to talk. So she danced and laughed and waved her arms as if she were having the time of her life. And in the small hours of Monday morning, when her eyes were gritty with tiredness, he took her back to the hotel suite.

He did not put the light on. Instead, as he closed the door behind them, he said quietly, 'Zoe—'

She did not mind him not putting the light on. As long as he put his arms round her and took her to bed. Tonight she wanted to take the same care of him that he had taken of her.

Hell, be honest, Zoe. You want a lot more than that.

Yes, but I want that, too.

Jay said in a strained voice, 'Zoe, this virginity thing. I didn't understand. I should have thought harder.'

Why didn't he put his arms round her?

'What do you mean?' she said, her voice slurring with tiredness. And lust. Well, more lust than tiredness. Probably.

'I don't think it was an accident that you were a virgin.'

'What?' Her head reared up. Suddenly she was not tired at all.

'You gave me a line about how it was just chance—boyfriends in different places, friends getting the wrong idea. I don't think it was anything to do with that. I think you were exactly what you should have been.'

She was so hurt she could not speak. Could hardly move. Everybody in the world thought she was a hot babe. Everybody but one. Jay Christopher thought she was meant to be alone.

'I should never have interfered.' His voice rasped.

'Well, you should know,' said Zoe, equally harsh.

She heard him swallow in the dark. 'I know. I'm sorry. Not much point in saying that now. But I am. I wish—oh, *hell*!'

And he left her to sleep alone.

Long after she had gone to bed Zoe heard him moving around in the sitting room. He was ultra-quiet. But her ears were strained for sounds that would tell her what he was doing. And they did.

He sat for a long while. By the window, she thought. In the dark, certainly, because there was no light under the connecting door. Then he got up and she heard him move a large piece of furniture, gently, carefully. Arranging the sofa, she realised.

So he wasn't intending to come back to bed. He must really have hated last night, then. She had made him break his every rule. Even making him hold her through the night. No, he was not going to forgive that.

He was going to take her back to England, employ her for one more week at Culp and Christopher—and then she was never going to see him again. It was inevitable. Zoe knew it now, though she had been pretending to herself all day. Trying to pretend, anyway.

She closed her eyes. Sleep was a long time coming.

Jay came into the bedroom very quietly the next morning. He was barefooted and walked cautiously. But Zoe was already awake. She struggled up on one elbow.

She was not going to let him see how he had hurt her last night. She was *not*. Fortunately there was good old Performance Zoe to call on in times of need.

'Time to go and lecture the masses?' she asked brightly.

His smooth dark hair was tousled, and he had a red line on his cheek where his night on the sofa's piped cushion had marked him. Zoe felt an almost irresistible urge to stroke it away. She was shocked, and pulled the sheet up to her chin.

Jay sent her an inscrutable look. 'There's no need to cower,' he said coldly. 'I didn't jump on you last night. I'm not going to do it this morning. I've got work to do.'

He disappeared into the bathroom, leaving Zoe shaken. She had never seen the cold come off him in waves like that before. Was that what the people at Culp and Christopher meant when they called him the Ice Volcano?

By the time she had dressed in her smart trousers and jacket Jay had packed. His bags stood by the door: overnight bag, laptop computer, briefcase. He was wearing one of his dark suits. The shirt this morning was silver-grey. Beautiful, of course, but much more sombre than usual. Maybe that was what made his eyes look lifeless. No green, no hazel. Just dark pools of emptiness.

There was no sunshine this morning. The canal was wreathed in fog and the doors to the hotel terrace were closed. So they breakfasted rapidly in the suffocating formality of the restaurant.

They hardly spoke. Jay was going through his notes one last time. When he did speak he was conscientiously pleasant. But it was clearly an effort.

He can't wait to get rid of me, thought Zoe. She felt as if he had struck her to the heart.

And then he gave her a gentle smile that did not seem as if it was an effort at all. For a moment her heart rose.

'I thought you'd like your last ride in a gondola. I've ordered one to take us to the conference hotel. Shame about the weather, though.'

But he did not touch her. Her heart sank back to the bottom of the ocean again.

Jay dealt with the practicalities swiftly. He paid the bill.

'We'll take our bags with us to the conference. That way we can circulate as long as possible before making a bolt for the airport.'

'Good thinking,' said Zoe, working hard to play bright and interested.

His smile was twisted. 'Just another thing I've done before.'

The mist had the odd effect of concentrating sound. In the gondola, Zoe could hear the plop and swish of the gondolier's pole, the lapping of water against the low sides of the boat. Her breathing. Jay's. But of the other gondolas, which loomed out of the mist and then were swallowed up again, she heard almost nothing. As they moved towards the Grand Canal, though, she heard the machine gun fire of the Vaporetti motors. And the mist swirled and pulled apart, getting thinner and thinner.

She thought, *This is the last time we'll ever be alone.*

She took Jay's hand quickly, before she lost her nerve.

She said in fierce, rapid under-voice, 'I want to say—I'm really glad it was you. I won't ever regret it.'

And then the gondolier poled them out between two tall palaces. And the mist dissolved into little puffballs of bite-sized cloud and they were into thin sunshine.

'Zoe—' Jay sounded strangled.

But the gondolier demanded clarification of their destination—and then the laptop overbalanced—and then another boat came dangerously close and a ferocious argument broke out. And then they were there.

He helped her up the steps. And held onto her hand when they were ashore, 'Zoe, we have to—I should have— Oh, hell, this is terrible timing.'

Zoe looked up and saw a man coming towards them along the canalside, hands held out in welcome.

'Jay. So good to have you. Come inside and meet everyone.'

Inevitably she slid into the background. Oh, everyone was kind—and Jay was meticulous in introducing her—but she had no role here. She could see it in everyone's eyes. They were tolerant, even intrigued. But the message was clear: she's just along for the ride.

Jay had her seated in the front row, though. He was doing his best to pretend that she was a fellow professional, thought Zoe, touched. The last thing he said to her before he disappeared onto the podium was, 'Now, don't forget to take notes. I want a proper post mortem on this speech.'

And her neighbour's smile said, as loudly as words, Yeah, yeah, yeah.

Zoe set her teeth and applied herself to the foolscap notepad.

Jay talked well. Not a surprise, of course. He was always fluent But this was different. He talked with knowledge and wit and ease. But also with a seriousness that was almost like passion.

He told the crowded room, 'Recently a friend reminded me that what we call public relations a lot of our critics call putting a spin on things.'

Zoe sat bolt upright. Jay smiled, straight at her.

'Not a high calling, you may think,' he went on. 'Not a very laudable role. Let me tell you what I think we do. And why it's important.'

There followed the stuff that she had researched. The statistics. The international examples. The anecdotes.

And then he said, 'When I first came into this business I was defensive. The press had stitched me up. I thought that what I was doing was giving people the tools to defend themselves against shallow and malignant journalism. But I have come to see that what we do is more than that. In our campaigns we are telling stories. We are reflecting the age back to itself. And in doing that—if we want to—we can reflect the best. Kindness instead of self-interest. Common humanity instead of hate. We are not just about selling things, ladies and gentlemen. We are about confirming values. In these dark days, that is important.'

He sat down to stunned silence. And then tumultuous applause. He did not take his eyes off Zoe's face.

Afterwards he was surrounded. The international delegates could hardly bear to leave him alone, it seemed. Four of them even insisted on accompanying Jay and Zoe back to the airport. In fact it was fortunate that they only had carry-on luggage or they would have missed the plane.

They whipped through formalities at top speed and were the last on the plane.

'What did you think of my talk?' said Jay.

But the noise of take-off was too great for easy conversation. And by the time they were airborne Zoe had thought better of saying, I thought you were talking only to me.

So she said lightly, 'It was great. You should have called it the death of spin.'

Her response did not please him.

'You and I,' said Jay grimly, 'are due a long talk.'

But the plane was not the place for it. Nor was the baggage hall. And when they got through customs and came out onto the crowded concourse the first person they saw was Molly di Paretti.

She blinked when she saw Zoe with Jay. But that did not stop her rushing over.

'Jay, bit of a crisis. We tried to get a message to the conference but you'd left. Barbara Lessiter has told a tabloid about your affair with Carla Donner. Banana is claiming that Carla only got her programme picked up by Sonnet Television because you're a director of Sonnet.'

Zoe stopped dead. His affair with Carla Donner? What affair?

She had never thought to ask about his private life. She had told him all about her own, spilled it out like the overgrown adolescent he clearly thought she was. It had not occurred to her that he might already be committed. He didn't *feel* committed.

But he wasn't saying, I'm not having an affair with Carla Donner. He was saying, exasperated, 'Banana Lessiter is a pain in the butt. Her eyelashes are bigger than her IQ.'

'We can't tell them that,' said Molly, walking rapidly beside him. She handed him a couple of sheets of closely typed paper. 'Sonnet are worried. An accusation like that could hold up their bid for American cable. They've got a press presentation tonight on the autumn schedules. We've planted a question. But you'll have to get a move on to make it. Car's here.'

'Good work,' said Jay, running hard eyes down Molly's list. 'Where's the presentation? No, don't bother. Better go straight there.'

They stormed through the concourse, talking hard. Zoe fell behind. Then slowed.

Finally she stopped.

Molly had talked about it as if everyone knew. Slowly Zoe accepted it. Jay was involved with Carla Donner! He probably thought Zoe already knew. Heaven help her, she would have already known, if she had had the wit to ask.

There had been plenty of rumours about his affairs in the office. Only she had never heard a name mentioned before. Now she had—Carla Donner was gorgeous and knowledgeable and as sophisticated as himself. Carla was the sort of woman he should have taken to Venice.

How stupid to think that Jay had been talking to her from the conference podium, thought Zoe. It was probably just another of his clever manipulative tricks. Find someone impressionable in the audience and play upon their feelings so they gave you all the feedback you needed.

'Zoe?'

She looked up.

Jay had come back for her. His eyes were still glittering with the light of anticipated battle and he looked harassed. But he was too well mannered just to walk off and leave her there, she thought.

'Are you coming?'

She swallowed, but her chin came up to the detonation angle.

'No, I don't think so. You've got a crisis to sort out. And I'm all dealt with, thank you,' she said clearly.

He looked astounded. 'Are you saying that's it? Thank you and goodnight?'

He sounded outraged, thought Zoe. She was pleased. That was the only thing that kept her from collapsing in the middle of Heathrow Terminal Two and bawling like an idiot.

'That's right. Thank you and goodnight,' she said, her eyes glittering as brilliantly as his own.

And before he could say a word she turned and bolted into the crowd.

Jay started to run after her. But he was just that half-second too late in setting off. The concourse was too crowded. He lost her before he had even taken a step.

He stopped. Took stock. Rushed out through the doors to see whether she was in the queue for taxis, but she was not there.

'Jay, come *on*,' said Molly, hopping from foot to foot beside an illegally parked limousine in front of the terminal building. The engine was running and a policeman was already approaching. 'The Sonnet press conference starts in forty minutes. We'll have to go like the clappers to get there anyway.'

He knew she was right.

He went.

It took hours. Every chance he could, he called Zoe on his mobile. He left message after message but he never made contact.

Eventually he got a faraway female voice which said, 'Zoe? Oh, no, she's not here. She's gone to Venice.'

'She's back,' he said curtly. 'That's why—'

The phone was clearly taken out of the vague woman's hand. 'I'm Artemis,' said a voice very like Zoe's. It sounded brisk.

The sister.

He said rapidly, 'I took her to Venice but we—got parted at the airport. I really, really need to speak to her.'

'If she went with you to Venice you've probably had your ration,' said Artemis cheerfully. 'No idea where she is. You could try Suze Manoir.'

'Right.' Why hadn't he thought of that? 'Thank you.'

'If you see her, tell her I'm sorry.'

'What?'

'None us had realised how bad Mother is. Zo's been doing all the work and hiding it from us. Now we've realised we're having a family conference. My father, Aunt Liz, Harry and me. The doctor's in with Dad and Aunt Liz now. Tell Zo she's off the hook.'

'Thank you,' said Jay, with real gratitude.

He rang off and called Suze's mobile.

'Yes, she's here,' said Suze, before he had even mentioned Zoe's name. 'And I don't know what you've done to her, you jerk, but I've never seen her look like that. Don't come near us.'

He did not accept it, of course. He went straight to the Edwardian block. He did not get past the front door.

'Go away,' snapped Suze down the entryphone. 'She's sleeping. She looks as if she hasn't slept for a week. You'll have to wait until tomorrow. I hope you're proud of yourself you—you—you Bluebeard.'

No, he was not proud of himself. But for all sorts of reasons that Suze Manoir could not guess at. He walked through the summer night, trying to wrestle his thoughts into some sort of order.

Women said that they loved men so easily, and most of the time it was just baiting the trap for long-term partnership.

But Zoe was not angling for companionship. She had her family. She had all those damned boyfriends. Now she could go out with any of them and do whatever she wanted in the full knowledge that she started off with a clean slate.

At the thought of Zoe doing whatever she wanted with another man Jay stopped dead and looked round for something to hit.

But then he reminded himself—before they went into that damned conference hall she had said she was glad that it was him. And that she would never regret it.

Well, she was regretting it now, all right. All because of that stupid Lessiter woman—

He caught himself. No, that wasn't true. It was his own fault. If he had sacked Barbara as soon as she'd developed her crazy crush on him, if he had never given his luke-warm affection to Carla, this would never have happened.

Zoe waited. Why couldn't I?

Hormones, thought Jay grimly, had a lot to answer for.

But hormones were only part of what he felt for Zoe Brown. Though God knows how he was ever going to convince her.

'My love,' he said experimentally to the warm night air.

And realised he had said it before. Holding her. Thinking only of her and her heart racing beneath him.

It had not felt like an experiment. It had felt like truth.

Slowly the tension went out of him. He'd got a hard task ahead, sure. But he'd had things too easy for too long. This was going to be a challenge—and worth it. This was the most important challenge of his life.

'My love,' Jay said again. With certainty.

CHAPTER TWELVE

'I CAN'T go to work,' Zoe said, panicking. 'I can't face him.'

Suze did not dignify that with an answer.

Zoe pulled herself together. 'I mean—I broke all his rules. He said I'd be out on the hour if I fell in love with him.'

'Are you in love with him?' said Suze curiously, buttering toast.

'Yes,' said Zoe baldly.

Suze bit back a gleeful smile. 'Then you'd better go in and let him sack you,' she advised.

Zoe gave a wan smile. 'Get it over as soon as possible if you're afraid of it? You're not the first to give me that advice.'

'And you're not the first to be afraid of Jay Christopher,' said Suze comfortingly.

But Zoe looked surprised. 'Oh, I'm not afraid of him.'

'Now that,' said Suze, handing her her jacket, '*is* a first.'

But Jay was not available when Zoe steadfastly called Blonde Mark II for a slot to see the boss.

'Don't think he'll be available all day,' said Poppy, kindly enough. 'Merger talks. You can try dropping by before you go home. He might be finished then.'

So Zoe did not see Jay. She *did* see—and would rather not have done—the unbelievably beautiful Bharati Christopher.

'Miss Brown,' said the tall, exquisitely dressed woman, pausing by Zoe's desk. 'Abby told me that was who you were. I am Jay's mother.'

She held out an expensively manicured hand. Zoe shook it as if she were in a dream.

'Hello, Mrs Christopher.'

'May I invite you to lunch?'

'Oh, no,' said Zoe with genuine horror.

Bharati looked rather pleased. 'Then show me where your water cooler is.'

Zoe leaped to her feet. 'This way.'

Bharati sipped cold water out of a plastic cup with all the elegance she would have accorded vintage champagne.

'So you won't talk to him,' she said musingly.

'I—er—' Zoe pulled herself together. 'What do you mean?'

'I am on a shopping trip. So I stay at my son's house. He was back very late last night. And very chastened.'

'Oh,' said Zoe.

'You seem to have him tied up in knots,' said Bharati Christopher dispassionately.

'Oh.'

'And while I would, of course, prefer that he were not tied up in general,' she went on in her gentle, precise voice, 'you are the first woman to have got close to Jay for years. Perhaps ever.' She put the plastic cup in the bin provided with great care. 'Don't waste it.'

Zoe was speechless.

Bharati left with a faint smile.

Zoe threw her head back. *'Aaaaaarrgh!'*

But it confirmed her resolve not to go home until she had seen him.

Was his mother right? The first woman to have got close to Jay! Was it possible?

And what about Carla Donner? Zoe had gone through every newspaper this morning and there had been no mention of the television gardener, let alone Jay's affair with her. Yet would his mother necessarily know?

She was torn all day. There was work to do, but Zoe was working on autopilot. She hardly noticed what she was doing. She got odd looks from Molly, but she did not seem to have told anyone else that she had met Zoe along with Jay at the airport, coming back from their weekend in Venice.

Kind Abby asked her whether she was feeling all right, though. Clearly Zoe's distraction was showing.

'Look,' said Abby, as everyone else began to drift away at the end of the day, 'you haven't had anything to eat all day. You haven't been out of the building. What's wrong?'

But Zoe just shook her head. 'I—er—think I'll get some coffee,' she said uneasily. 'Poppy said there was always a pot on the go for Jay in her office.'

'Good idea,' said Abby, unsuspecting. She pushed her sunglasses on top of her head and hiked up her shoulder bag. 'Don't stay too late. It's a beautiful summer night. Everyone ought to be out looking at the stars.'

Fat chance, thought Zoe.

But she went bravely up to Jay's office.

Poppy had obviously gone. Her desk was tidy and nearly empty. The room was quiet, but the air was full of the luscious smell of Jay's favourite coffee. Zoe helped herself, skirted the man-eating plant and opened the door to his office. Jay's desk was equally clear.

She bit her lip. Looked as if he wasn't coming back tonight, then. She ought to go, but somehow she was reluctant to leave the place where he spent most of his days.

She wandered round the room, sipping her coffee, touching the surfaces, pulling books off the bookshelf, running her hands voluptuously down the upholstery of his chair, where his shoulders habitually rested. She brushed her cheek against the top of the tall chair.

'Jay,' she said aloud. All her longing was in it. All her love.

The door banged back. She looked up.

Jay stood in the doorway. She hardly recognised him. His face looked fleshless, as if he had been running. His eyes were concentrated and intent.

'So you're here,' he said in a still voice.

Zoe straightened rapidly. 'Thought I'd save you the bother of summoning me,' she said in a bright voice.

He frowned. 'Summoning you?'

'You're going to kick me out, right?' she said, quite as if she didn't care. 'After Venice? House rules?'

But her heart cried, Touch me. Love me.

'Oh, that.' He sounded almost bored. 'I suppose so.'

He *supposed* so?

'Well, don't give yourself a heart attack,' said Zoe, hurt. 'I'm sorry I have made so little impact on Culp and Christopher.'

He gave a snort of bitter laughter. 'Culp and Christopher? What about the impact you've made on me?'

She stared, clutching his chair like a shield. 'What?'

He was carrying a briefcase. He flung it away from him, into the corner of the room, as savagely as if he was launching a spear.

'Right. You're sacked. Satisfied?'

'The agency—'

'The agency will survive,' said Jay between rigid lips. 'I'm not sure I will.'

'Wha-at?'

He took a hasty step forward. 'I love you,' he said intensely. 'I never said that to anyone before. But I said it to you without even thinking.'

'You—did—not.'

'Yes, I did. I called you my love. What else do you think that was?' His eyes narrowed. 'Or do all your men call you that?'

Zoe decided that now was not the time to ask him to define his terms. She had never seen a man closer to breaking point.

'Well, if they did they didn't mean it.'

'Oh, God.' He sounded frantic. 'I don't know what to do about this. Your sister says I've had my ration. Susan Manoir said I'd hurt you. I keep thinking I'm too old for you—'

Zoe stopped hanging onto his chair like a lifeline and stepped round the desk.

'Why don't you ask me?' she said gently.

He shut his eyes. 'Will you marry me?'

She gave a soft laugh. His eyes flew open.

'Only on one condition,' said Zoe, hot babe incarnate.

His eyes questioned wildly.

She laughed softly and moved in close. 'You take me home and make love to me *now*.'

It was a perfect summer night. His room was huge and airy, windows open to the night-time sounds of birds and small animals. The moonlit breeze was cool on her skin, like a lover's breath.

I know what a lover's breath on my skin feels like now.

They had left their clothes behind them, in the hallway, on the stairs. Zoe trembled to his slightest touch.

There was only one doubt left in her mind.

'Why did you say that it was not chance that I was a virgin?'

He curved his hand round her neck, kissing her skin with moth wing dabs. Her lips parted and her breath quickened—and he relished it.

'Mmm?' he said, concentrating.

'Why did you say that it wasn't chance?'

He paused reluctantly, though his hand started to do wickedly enticing things to her nipple.

'Your family,' he said, surprised. 'When you told me about your mother it was so clear. You'd watched her collapse because your father left. You must have thought, This is grown-up stuff and I'm not ready for it. Perfectly sensible.'

'Oh.'

Zoe was not feeling sensible. She was feeling wanton and wonderful.

She said, 'I never thought of that. I just thought sex was mostly hormones and showing off.'

Jay gave a shaken laugh. 'And now?'

Zoe took hold of the wickedly skilful hand at her breast and carried it lower, to where they both had everything to discover.

'Now I know it,' she said coolly. 'And, oh, boy, have I got some showing off to do.'

But he made her wait. 'Not until you admit there's a little matter of love involved as well.'

He watched her eyes darken and nearly lost his resolve. But this was important. And he was good at physical self-control.

Her head fell back. 'Love…'

He stroked her so slowly that her eyes crossed.

'I don't know what love is,' she moaned.

'Yes, you do.'

He saw her bite her tongue as she tried to hold on to her senses.

'Okay, okay,' she said breathlessly. 'I fell in love with you at first sight. I thought you looked like a Mogul prince and I knew you were for me. I wanted you to make love to me, but I wanted you to talk to me and live with me and listen to me for the rest of our lives as well.'

Jay was humbled. He said so.

Zoe writhed. 'Good,' she gasped. 'I hope that's everything you want. Because I don't think I can hang on much longer...'

'Everything,' said Jay. 'Except maybe...'

Their bodies slid together in a slow, voluptuous locking. Somehow it took them into another dimension. He saw her eyes widen and widen as she realised it, too. For a moment he held her very still, looking deeply into her eyes. No reservations. No disguise.

Her lips parted. 'I love you.' She framed the words soundlessly, as if she were talking direct to his spirit. Her eyes were honest. All guards down now.

'Yes,' said Jay.

And took her on a journey he'd thought he knew by heart—and found he had never travelled it before.

Later they lay entwined in the dark. From his pillow they could see the fuzzy moon above the trees.

'What would you have done if I hadn't come looking for you?' said Zoe.

She could feel his smile against her skin. At once she detected teasing. She knew him so well now.

'What?'

Jay did not take his possessive hand off her naked waist. 'I was going to try and bribe you,' he said lazily.

'Don't believe it.'

Still keeping one hand on her, he stretched a long arm and extracted what he was looking for from a pocket in one of the garments on the floor. He flicked it across the bed.

'I spent today cancelling the merger. I thought I'd rather stay small and keep my self-respect,' he said. 'You taught me that. So I thought it would please you.'

It was a little velvet pouch. Zoe fingered it, but it was of less importance than what he was saying.

'I taught *you*?' She hardly dared to believe it.

'My darling.' He stroked her hair behind her ear. 'I love the way your curls cling to my fingers.'

'Electricity,' said Zoe impatiently. 'What do you mean, I taught you?'

'Love that electricity.' Jay gathered her close. For all the teasing laughter in his voice, Zoe knew this was serious. 'You saw right through my protective colouring right from the start,' he told her. 'Then, in Venice, you went further. You saw the man I'd forgotten was there.'

'Oh!' Her eyes filled. 'Oh, *Jay*.'

He unlaced the pouch. Stones fell out, heavy and warm and gleaming faintly in the darkness.

'Very useful, your not having any jewellery,' he said lightly. 'When we're old we can take up collecting rubies as a hobby. But for now—'

It was a necklace. She turned it over. In the light of the moon she saw the sheen.

'Do they solidify silk, somehow?' she said doubtfully.

He switched on the bedside light. The necklace was made of enamels—turquoise and rose and peacock and flame. The colours of his fantastic shirts. The colours of his imagination.

The colours of his life.

'Put it on for me,' she said softly.

His fingers were not entirely steady.

She ran her hands all over the compact and elegant body. She had, she thought exultantly, the right now. She was his and he was hers.

She leaned over him, her hair catching the light. It was as soft as silk against that wonderful golden skin. They gave a sigh of exquisite longing at exactly the same moment.

'And now, my Mogul Prince, my darling,' said Zoe, 'love me.'